She was beautiful, but it wasn't her looks that kept his eyes riveted on her.

There was something there, just beneath the surface, that he could almost remember. He hadn't felt that about any of the other people from his forgotten life.

"Will you help me to remember it?" he asked quietly. "That life with my wife. My daughters."

"I wasn't here for most of that part."

"What about our friendship? I have a feeling that you mattered to me, too."

"Yes. But Mia was the one who deserved you."

What did that mean? He was about to ask, but then one of the toddlers threw a plastic cup across the kitchen, breaking the moment. Sawyer and Olivia both looked in that direction, and Sawyer cleared his throat.

"It's a lot to ask to help a man get his memory back, I know...but I need help."

"I'll do what I can," she agreed.

"Thank you." And he meant it from the bottom of his aching heart. For the first time in his limited memory, he felt something close to comfort.

Patricia Johns writes from Alberta, Canada. She has her Hon. BA in English literature and currently writes for Harlequin's Love Inspired and Heartwarming lines. You can find her at patriciajohnsromance.com.

Books by Patricia Johns

Love Inspired

Montana Twins

Her Cowboy's Twin Blessings
Her Twins' Cowboy Dad
A Rancher to Remember

Comfort Creek Lawmen

Deputy Daddy
The Lawman's Runaway Bride
The Deputy's Unexpected Family

His Unexpected Family
The Rancher's City Girl
A Firefighter's Promise
The Lawman's Surprise Family

Harlequin Heartwarming

A Baxter's Redemption
The Runaway Bride
A Boy's Christmas Wish
Her Lawman Protector

Visit the Author Profile page
at Harlequin.com for more titles.

A Rancher to Remember

Patricia Johns

HARLEQUIN LOVE INSPIRED®

Recycling programs
for this product may
not exist in your area.

LOVE INSPIRED BOOKS

ISBN-13: 978-1-335-42898-1

A Rancher to Remember

www.Harlequin.com

Printed in U.S.A.

Blessed are they that mourn:
for they shall be comforted.
—*Matthew* 5:4

To my husband, the love of my life.
Every year with you gets sweeter.

Chapter One

Olivia Martin pulled to a stop in front of the low ranch house, squinting against the late afternoon sunlight. She turned off her car and got out. The spring breeze was chilly, but the sunlight was welcomingly warm. She slipped on her leather jacket, and did a full turn, taking in the newly green fields to the west and the wooden fence that separated the house from the rest of the ranch. A beaten-up Chevy pickup was parked by the house, and the screen door was propped open. A child's babble filtered out of the open door— a squeal, and then a laugh.

Olivia wouldn't have come back to Beaut,

if it weren't for the crushing debt that her mother's battle with cancer had left hanging over her and her brother. She had her own reasons for steering clear of this town, but it wasn't just about her. Her brother, Brian, had stayed in Beaut after their mother's death, burdened by a debt load that had stalled his life completely, leaving a tense bitterness between them. If her brother was going to have anything to do with her again, she needed to find a financial solution that would help him out. But the solution she'd found all depended on her old friend Sawyer West.

Olivia didn't expect to find Sawyer at the house in the middle of the day. He was employed here at his uncle's ranch, after all, and she'd figured he'd be out in a field somewhere. But standing by the fence, a boot hooked on the lowest rung and his hat pushed back on his head, was a familiar figure. She couldn't see his face from where she stood, but she'd know Sawyer anywhere. A smile came to her lips as she sent up a silent prayer of thanks. Maybe this would be easier than she thought, because she sure had been praying hard for some success here with Sawyer.

"Sawyer!" she called. He didn't move, and she started toward him, her boots crunching against gravel until she hit the grass. "Sawyer!"

He turned then, slowly and deliberately. He'd always been a good-looking guy and that hadn't changed, but he'd hardened over the last two years since his wife's death. Those laughing brown eyes had become flinty and cautious, and he seemed to have more scruff on his chin now than he used to wear before. She knew that the last couple of years had been hard on him… There was a white bandage on the side of his forehead, looking out of place. His level gaze landed on her, but his expression didn't change.

"Hi!" Olivia felt her smile falter. "Sorry to just drop in like this, but—"

Sawyer looked at her quizzically, then his gaze slid past her toward the house.

"Sawyer?" she said.

"Who are you?" he said uncertainly.

Was he joking? But there was no hint of humor in those chiseled features. Something was very wrong here. She heard the screen door slam behind her and glanced over her shoulder to see Lloyd West, Sawyer's uncle, sauntering toward her, carrying a blonde toddler in each arm. Lloyd was an awkwardly proportioned man. He had long arms and legs, hands and feet that seemed too big for the rest of his body, a sparsely whiskered face, a totally bald pate and a large nose. The toddlers seemed to be taking a real delight in trying to reach up and touch his shiny head.

"I know I probably should have called first, but I wanted to surprise you," Olivia said, turning back to Sawyer. She smiled sheepishly. "Surprise."

Sawyer smiled weakly, still eyeing her uncertainly. "You know me?"

Olivia blinked. Was he being serious right now? No, surely not. So why the act? Was he angry still? She licked her lips.

"I know it's been a while, Sawyer, but come on. This is just cruel."

Lloyd arrived then, and he put the toddlers down. One went for Sawyer's leg, and the other squatted down to pick grass.

"Olivia," Lloyd said with a lopsided smile that revealed a gap where he'd lost a tooth. He stuck out his hand. They shook, and Lloyd looked toward his nephew. "Do you remember her?"

"No." Sawyer's voice was low. "I've got nothing."

"This is Olivia Martin. She's an old friend." Sawyer gave her a curt nod. "Pleasure."

"What do you mean?" Olivia's mind was spinning. "Lloyd, what's going on?" Her gaze stopped at the little girls. They had bright blue eyes, identical smiles and curls that had been gathered into nubby little pigtails at the sides of their heads. These would be Sawyer's daughters—the reason Sawyer's in-laws were so eager to reconcile with him to begin with. Even as she looked at Lloyd for some sort of explanation, she knew it couldn't happen in front of the girls.

Taking the hint, Lloyd angled his head toward the house and took a step back, and Olivia followed him a few paces off. Sawyer watched them for a moment, then scooped the toddler into his arms and turned back toward the field.

"Sawyer was in an accident a couple of days ago," Lloyd said, keeping his voice low. "He got kicked in the head by a cow when he was trying to put the chains on her for a difficult delivery. He was unconscious for about five minutes, and when he came to… this." Lloyd sighed.

"What is *this*?" Olivia demanded.

"Temporary amnesia. He doesn't remember anything. We took him to the hospital and they did a bunch of tests. The doctor says his memory should come back here pretty soon, so right now, it's just a waiting game."

"So Sawyer doesn't remember me?" she asked hesitantly.

"Don't take it personally," Lloyd replied with a shrug. "He doesn't remember me, either. Or his girls."

She watched as the toddler who was playing in the grass headed in her father's direction. Sawyer put down the other girl, and they both reached for their father and clutched at his jeans. He smoothed a hand over the tops of their heads but didn't lean down to pick them up again.

"How long does it normally take to get memory back with his kind of injury?" she asked.

"A week or two, the doctor says," Lloyd replied. "The damage isn't too bad. It could have been a lot worse. But it's good you're here. Maybe you can jostle a few memories loose for him."

Olivia smiled wanly. "If his own daughters aren't enough... Maybe with Mia gone, he doesn't want to remember."

Mia was Sawyer's late wife, and Sawyer and Mia had been Olivia's best friends, but that was a long time ago.

"Well, his girls need their father to come back to himself," Lloyd retorted. "So, he'd better start pulling up a few memories, no matter how painful they might be."

Olivia pulled her fingers through her sandy blond curls. Her mind was spinning. She was here to try and mend fences between Sawyer and his in-laws. Mia's parents, Wyatt and Irene White, had made her a deal: if she could soften Sawyer up enough to allow them access to their granddaughters, then they'd use their clout with the hospital board to help reduce the medical bills from her mother's illness. The weight of that debt had been the reason her brother wouldn't speak to her anymore. One reconciled family for another—that was the deal. But the timing couldn't be worse. If Sawyer couldn't remember anything, how could he reconcile with the Whites? But then again, if he couldn't remember, maybe he'd be okay with them visiting the girls, after all.

Using his amnesia that way was underhanded, and she knew it. Olivia was an honest woman, and she wasn't willing to manipulate an already vulnerable situation, no matter how high the stakes were. Sawyer's memory would come back. That's what the doctors said, right? She could hold off on convincing him until then.

One of the toddlers drummed her hands against Sawyer's leg and started to cry. He bent down and picked her up then, and she tipped her curly head against his shoulder. He patted her back awkwardly, murmuring something to her that Olivia couldn't make out.

"The problem is," Lloyd went on, "we're real busy right now what with calving and all. Sawyer being out of it has slowed us down, and I've had to stick around the house to watch him and the girls, so that sets me back even further."

"Yes, I could see that being tough," she agreed.

"How long are you out here for?" Lloyd asked.

Olivia had two weeks off of work at the hospital in Billings, and she wasn't planning on staying a day longer than it took to iron things out around here. But there was slim chance of a reconciliation happening by then if Sawyer couldn't remember anything.

"A couple of weeks, I suppose," she replied.

"Because if you'd be willing to pitch in here with Sawyer, keep an eye on the kids a bit—"

"Who normally watches them?" she asked with a frown.

"Ellen Guise was their nanny. One of our relatives. But yesterday, she got a call from her daughter. Some sort of emergency with her mother-in-law in Tennessee. So she had to go," Lloyd said. "I mean, she'll be back in a few weeks, but it's just tough timing all round. Look, the thing is, I can't offer to pay you or anything. I'm in a real bind. Everyone else is as busy as I am with their own cattle, so I don't have anywhere else to turn right now. It would free me up to get back to work. I'm just asking as a favor. I mean, if you had the time, or something. Besides, maybe you can help him to remember."

Lloyd met her gaze pleadingly, and he rubbed a hand over his bald head. Then he let his hand drop to his side.

She'd come back to Beaut for two things: to try and reconcile Sawyer to his late wife's family, and to do a little reconciling of her own with her brother. She couldn't do either of those things until Sawyer was back to himself. When she needed his help so badly, how could she turn down the chance to help him in turn? Besides, this was Sawyer. She had some hard memories in this town, and she didn't trust people to have changed a whole lot. But Sawyer had been one of the good ones. She sighed, glancing back at the rugged cowboy by the fence. She'd have to help him—she knew that.

"Do you think Sawyer wants me here?" she asked quietly.

"It's all the same to him, I think," Lloyd said. "At first, he was pretty freaked out, not remembering anything. Now he just seems like he's given up. Stands there and looks out at the fields. I can't let him come with me like this—he's another accident waiting to happen. He needs someone to hang out with him, remind him of things."

"Well… I do need to try and sort a few things out with my brother while I'm here," she said. "But I could pitch in. For a few days, at least."

"Would you?" Lloyd asked, a relieved smile breaking over his face. "Olivia, you have no idea how much that would help me. I don't want to push you into anything, of course…"

"No, no, I'm happy to help," she said.

"Thank you. Would it put you out too much to live here? I know you probably have something else arranged, but it would be great if you could stay in the house with us. I've got an office on the opposite end of the house from where me and Sawyer sleep. There's a single bed in there. So it'll be comfortable enough for you, and feel free to eat whatever you want from the fridge…"

"No problem," Olivia said. "I've got a room booked at the hotel in town, but I can cancel that." She'd help where she could, make some time to try to visit with her brother, and maybe by the time she left, Sawyer would be back to normal and he'd be willing to sit down with his late wife's parents and make peace. God worked in mysterious ways, and perhaps this was all part of a bigger plan.

She could only hope. Because right now, her biggest priority was her relationship with her brother, and if she couldn't offer him some sort of reprieve from their troubles, she doubted that he'd want anything to do with her again.

Sawyer looked down at the curly-headed toddler in his arms, and he struggled to latch on to a memory…any memory, but he came up empty. He hated this helpless, confused feeling, knowing these little girls were expecting something from him that he didn't know how to give.

"Daddy." She blinked at him, her big blue eyes fixed on his face hopefully. What she wanted from him, he wasn't sure. He'd

known these children for two days now, and
everything before that was darkness. They
seemed to know him well enough. Just like
everyone else around here. Ranch hands, his
uncle, doctors…they all called him Sawyer,
which was his name, apparently, except for
these little cuties. His heart softened just
looking at them… They called him Daddy.

Sawyer couldn't tell them apart. Lloyd told
him that they were named Elizabeth and Is-
abella, or Lizzie and Bella for short. And
they adored him and relied on him. They
clambered into his lap, played with his shirt
pockets and carried him a fresh diaper when
they needed a change. The first time they'd
done that, he'd been stunned, but Lloyd had
assured him that this was his job. He was
their dad, after all. And apparently, Lloyd
wasn't keen on diaper duty.

There wasn't a mother in the picture. Sawyer had asked about that, and Lloyd had
filled him in that his wife had died in child-
birth. He didn't remember his wife. Lloyd
had dug out a wedding album, and he'd seen

smiling people he didn't recognize. Even the groom seemed like a stranger to him. The bride didn't ring any bells, either. But she was pretty, and he knew he must have loved her by the look on his face in those pictures.

Lloyd and the young woman started walking toward him again. She was pretty, too, but in a different way from the bride in the photos. Olivia—wasn't that what Lloyd had called her? She was relaxed, wearing jeans over the tops of her boots, and a blouse with a leather jacket on top of it all. Her hair was loose and curly, a dark blond color, and when her gaze met his, he noted the dark brown of her eyes.

"So, Olivia is going to stay with us for a few days," Lloyd said as they approached.

"Oh, yeah?" Sawyer raised an eyebrow.

"I understand that you don't remember me, but I'm—" Olivia swallowed, her gaze moving down to the toddler at his knees, then snapping back up to his face. "I'm your friend. We've got quite a history, and I was actually coming back to town to see you. So, if I can help out, I want to. I mean, if you'd be comfortable with me here..."

Sawyer shrugged. "Suit yourself."

There was something about her—something almost comforting—that tickled in the back of his mind. But even without that, he understood why Lloyd wanted her to stay. Sawyer knew that he was in the way here at the house, on the ranch...everywhere. Lloyd was antsy, and he had other things he'd rather be doing than babysitting some confused cowboy who didn't know his boots from his teakettle.

But I'm a cowboy, he thought to himself. Lloyd had told him that, and it felt right, somehow.

"I've got to get back out to the fields," Lloyd said. "And Olivia can help with the girls."

"Yeah, that would be great..." Sawyer didn't mean to sound quite so relieved, but he was in over his head with Lizzie and Bella. He might be their dad, but that biological fact didn't seem to be much help right now. "Look, I don't remember anything… you included."

"Lloyd filled me in," she replied. "But your injury isn't supposed to be permanent, so maybe while I'm here, I can help you remember a few things."

"Did you know their mother?" he asked, glancing down at the toddlers.

"I was Mia's best friend," she said with a sad smile. "And yours, once upon a time. We three were inseparable there for a while. I was a bridesmaid at your wedding."

"Oh." He nodded. "I saw the photos, but you probably look different out of that frilly dress."

"Yeah, I would." She smiled.

So maybe she'd be an authoritative source for information. "Okay. You sure you don't have better things to do?"

"Not really." She shrugged. "You wouldn't remember my brother, Brian, but he's the only family I've got in town, so…"

"So, we're settled then?" Lloyd interrupted, glancing at his watch. "Because if

I could get out to the fields and pitch in tonight, it would make it easier on the rest of the guys."

"Yes," Olivia said, shooting Lloyd a smile. "Do what you need to do. We'll be fine."

"And you're okay with this, right?" Lloyd asked him.

Sawyer shrugged. "Sure."

It wasn't like he remembered any of them right now, anyway. Olivia sounded rather confident, and maybe that was a good thing.

"Okay. Well, I'm going to head out for a couple of hours, and then I'll come back and check in with you," Lloyd said. He pulled a piece of paper and the nub of a pencil out of his pocket. He tore off a corner and scribbled on it. "That's my cell number if you need me."

"Thanks." She looked at it, then tucked it into her pocket.

Lloyd gave them both a nod, then headed over to the pickup truck. Was it just him, or did Lloyd look like he was just about running to get out of here? Sawyer wasn't sure he blamed him.

"I guess that leaves just us," Sawyer said. "I feel like I should apologize for this."

"Whatever," she said. "It isn't your fault."

"No, but it's highly inconvenient," he replied. "Apparently, I usually work here. A lot of use I am like this."

"You're Lloyd's nephew," she said with a shake of her head. "You're family."

"Right." He wished that meant more to him right now.

Sawyer scooped up one toddler then looked down at the child attached to his leg. He kept his leg straight, lifting her along with him as he headed back toward the house. The toddler squealed in delight, and he couldn't help but laugh softly.

"So, one of them is Lizzie, and the other is Bella. I haven't figured out which is which yet," he said. "Do you know, by any chance?"

"I last saw your girls when they were newborns," Olivia replied. "So I'm not much help. Wait—" She reached out toward the toddler in his arms and took her hand. "What's your name, sweetie?"

"Lizzie…" the girl whispered. Olivia shot him a grin, and then bent down to the other toddler. "Is your name Bella?"

The other girl grinned impishly. "Lizzie!"

Olivia straightened and laughed softly. "Never mind. I thought I was onto something."

"I tried that," he admitted. "And Lloyd says he can't tell them apart, either. When we figure it out, I'm going to have to mark them somehow."

"What…like with a permanent marker?" she asked, shooting him a teasing look.

"You're joking, but it's not a bad idea," he countered. "Apparently, I could tell them apart before, but now…" Sadness welled up inside of him, and he tried to push it back. "They say it'll come back to me. Until it does, a nice *B* or *L* on their hands would be helpful."

Sawyer disentangled the little girl from his

leg, and then put his other daughter on the ground next to her. They scampered on ahead.

"Do you remember the accident?" Olivia asked.

"No," he said. "The first thing I remember is waking up with blood on my face, and riding to the hospital in town. I don't remember anything before it."

"Nothing?" she asked, squinting over at him.

He shook his head. "Well, I mean, I remember some funny little things, like which cupboard holds the salt shaker. If I'm not thinking about it, I can go through the motions for some basic chores like washing dishes or making coffee."

"So, the muscle memories are in there," she said.

"Seems like," he agreed.

"I'm a nurse, you know," she said. "I work in an emergency room, and I've dealt with people with partial memory loss after a head injury, but never anything this complete. In the cases I've worked with, the patients usually get their memories back within a couple of hours."

"Yeah?" He eyed her curiously. Maybe she could be helpful after all.

"What did the doctors tell you—exactly?"

"It's a brain injury. Kind of like a bruise. But it isn't getting worse, and it should heal in a week or two. My memory should return. They said they've seen it before."

"Okay, that's a good sign," she said with a nod. "I'm sure relaxing a bit will help with that."

He shot her a rueful look. "Try relaxing when the most important parts of your life have been erased from your head. Besides— I want to get out there. Do something. Feel useful."

"That's your way," she said with a low laugh.

"What do you mean?"

"You like to work. You always did. You worked harder than any cowboy here."

That wasn't a bad thing. He smiled at the description. "It could be worse."

"You need to relax," she said, and her tone wasn't amused.

The toddlers stopped at the steps of the house and turned around, heading back toward them. Their curls bounced as they ran, and one of them came straight for Olivia. She bent down and swept the girl up in her arms, planting her on her hip. The move was so natural that he found himself smiling at her.

Sawyer caught the second girl, and picked her up, too. It was easier with two adults. They weren't outnumbered, and Olivia seemed more natural with the girls than Sawyer was.

"What's your name?" Olivia asked brightly.

"Bella."

"Yeah, you're Bella?"

"Bella."

Sawyer looked at the toddler in his arms. "Hey, Lizzie," he said softly.

"Daddy..."

Sawyer looked over at Olivia, his heart speeding up. "Did we just do it?"

"I think we know who's who," she agreed.

"Okay, don't put her down," Sawyer said, waggling a finger at Olivia. "We're finding a marker."

"That was a joke," she laughed.

"It was a good idea. I need to tell them apart."

Sawyer led the way up the steps and into the side door of the ranch house. He might not remember much, but he did have a mental picture in his mind of a junk drawer of some sorts that had a big felt-tipped marker inside. He looked around the kitchen, unsure of where to start, so he began at the first drawer he saw, pulling it open, then closing it when it wasn't the right one. On the fifth drawer, he found it.

"There we go." He pulled out the marker with a grin. "If there were a mother I'd have to explain myself to, I might be a little more worried. But I'm their dad, right?"

"So I've been told," she replied with a small smile.

"Yeah, well, as their dad, I figure telling them apart is pretty important. I need something that won't just wash off."

"Okay."

"So I'm making a responsible parenting decision here." He held up the marker, watching her for a reaction.

"You're their dad," she said with a nod. "It's your call."

While he didn't remember anything about them, being their father still mattered. In fact, as confused as he was, focusing on being their father had been what had held him together so far.

Sawyer pulled off the cap and took Lizzie's hand. He wrote a small L on the back of her hand, and then blew on it to dry the ink. Lizzie looked down at her hand in curiosity, and he put her down on the kitchen floor, then reached for Bella's hand. She held hers out happily, and he wrote a small B.

Bella pursed her lips to try and blow, and

he laughed, then blew on her hand to make sure the ink was dry.

"There," he said. "That's one problem solved."

It felt good—a victory. Olivia put Bella down, and the girls scampered off to a bucket of toys in the corner and dumped it out. He watched them for a moment... It still felt unreal that he was a father and that these little girls were actually his.

"What was I like?" he asked, glancing toward Olivia.

"You were serious," Olivia said. "And stubborn. Really stubborn. You knew what you wanted and you didn't let anything get in your way. You wanted to help your uncle grow this ranch—you thought you could double the herd size with the right support."

"Hmm." A goal. He liked the sound of that. "How did you and I know each other?"

"We met at the diner where I was working. We just kind of...clicked. It went from there."

"And you live in town still?" he asked.

"No, I moved for college," she said. "Right after you got married. I live in Billings now. I work at the hospital there."

He frowned slightly, taking her in—the tangled curls, the soft brown eyes, the pink in her cheeks. "What was my wife like?"

Olivia's expression froze, and then she glanced away.

"Perfect for you," she replied. "Mia loved horses and cattle. She wanted a ranch life. And she was quiet enough to balance you out."

"I take it you didn't want the ranch life like we did," he said. "Since you moved."

"I wanted…" She looked around the kitchen, her gaze turning inward. "I didn't want to stick around Beaut. I guess I just wanted more." She winced. "That sounds insulting. I don't mean it to be. I just didn't want a rural life. I wanted a new start. I wanted…streetlights and a nightlife, and more people. I was tired of living in a place where everyone knew my personal business, or thought they did."

She was beautiful, but it wasn't her looks that kept his eyes riveted to her. There was something there, just beneath the surface, that he could almost remember. He hadn't felt that about any of the other people from his forgotten life that he'd met so far. But he had a foggy memory—a black coat and a woman facing away from him. He put out his hand and touched her. She turned—

Then nothing. He couldn't get any more of it, but it felt connected to her. Or was the memory of his wife and talking to a woman bringing it back? He couldn't tell. Not remembering was a strange weight. He was sad—or was that sadness some part of a memory that he couldn't place, like the woman in the black coat? He wished he knew. It was confusing and frustrating. All he had was these shards of memory that didn't fit anywhere, and sadness so deep that it made his chest sore.

"Will you help me to remember it?" he asked quietly. "That life with my wife. My daughters."

"I wasn't here for most of that part," she said with a quick shake of her head.

"Right…" So she might not be able to help with that as much as he'd hoped, but still, when he looked at her, that memory of the coat kept brushing so close that he could almost touch it. "What about our friendship? I have a feeling that you mattered to me, too."

Olivia blinked up at him and she opened her mouth to say something, then stopped.

"*Did* you matter to me?" he asked. He needed to know that much.

She nodded. "Yes. But Mia was the one who deserved you."

What did that mean? He was about to ask, but then one of the toddlers threw a plastic cup across the kitchen and it clattered into a corner, breaking the moment. Sawyer and Olivia both looked in that direction, and Sawyer cleared his throat.

"It's a lot to ask to help a man get his memory back, I know…but I need help."

"I'll do what I can," she agreed.

"Thank you." And he meant it from the

bottom of his aching heart. For the first time in his limited memory, he felt something close to comfort.

Chapter Two

It was odd to be standing here with a man she'd known for so long, talking like virtual strangers. Sawyer wasn't quite the same as Olivia remembered him. She figured that would still be true even if his mind was fully intact. He might not have his memory, but these last hard years hadn't been erased; she could see that in the lines on his face and the strands of premature gray around his temples.

Sawyer crossed the kitchen to the coffee maker and reached for a stack of filters. Olivia watched him work for a moment. He'd bulked up a bit since the last time she'd seen

him, making him move with more confidence. His hands—she noticed them as he
fiddled with a coffee filter—looked tougher,
more calloused. He glanced instinctively toward the toddlers, who sat in the middle of
a plastic minefield of toys.

"You used to like baseball," Olivia said.

"Did I?" Sawyer glanced over his shoulder. "Playing it or watching it?"

"Both," she replied. "You played in high
school, at least, but that was before I was
in high school, and before we properly met.
You're older than me by a couple of years,
by the way."

"Right." He smiled.

"We used to play catch in the park, you
and me. When you weren't working. You
worked a lot."

"Did you play baseball, too?" he asked.

Olivia would have…but there had been
some women who'd liked to play with the
local team who'd been part of spreading
those rumors about her, and avoiding them
had been simpler and less painful than stand-

ing her ground and facing them down. At that point she'd been so tired from the constant badgering around town, that she'd just let people believe what they wanted to about her. If they wanted to think she was sleeping around, then so be it, because no one was listening to her anyway. It was easier in the moment, at least. But it had confirmed that getting out of Beaut was the only option she had.

"No, I wasn't into baseball," she said. It wasn't entirely true—but it wasn't really a lie. Joining the team would have been fun under different circumstances, but all she had was reality, not a fairy tale. And in her reality, baseball hadn't been right for her at all.

"Huh." Sawyer cast her a peculiar look, then turned back to making the coffee again.

"Why?" she asked. "Do you remember something?"

"No, you just really tensed up when you said you weren't into baseball," he replied. "What's up with that?"

"Stuff I'd rather forget," she said, forcing a smile, then nodded toward the coffee maker. "You remember how to make coffee."

Sawyer nodded. "I realized that yesterday. How did I take my coffee when you knew me?"

"How have you been taking it so far?" she asked.

He screwed the lid back onto the coffee canister. "Lloyd has been handing it to me black." He flicked the button on the coffee maker and turned back toward her. "I've been following suit when I make it myself. Is that how I liked it?"

Olivia shrugged. "When I knew you, you used to take a dribble of cream and about five spoons of sugar."

He frowned slightly. "That sounds gross. Are you sure?"

"Maybe you changed how you took it," she suggested. "I mean, maybe you started worrying about your health."

Or maybe Mia had started worrying about

it. Olivia couldn't speak for what had happened in his marriage.

"I'll try it both ways," Sawyer said. "Maybe you're right."

And maybe she wasn't... She'd adored Sawyer, but had she known him as well as she thought?

"How much did you and I hang out?" Sawyer asked.

Was he thinking the same thing?

"Quite a bit, back in the day," she said. "After you graduated, a lot of your friends had left for the city, and I didn't have a lot of friends anymore, besides Mia. So you and I kind of bonded over the lack of other options."

"That doesn't sound like a great foundation." But a smile tugged up the corner of his lips. "What do you mean, *anymore*? What happened to your friends?"

"I wasn't terribly popular," she hedged. "I was quiet. Kind of boring. And senior year, everyone decided to pick on me."

"Oh…" His gaze filled with sympathy. "I'm sorry."

"It *was* a good thing, in a roundabout way," she countered. "For us, at least. We might not have given each other much of a chance if we'd had other options. We wanted opposite things out of life, so we were a bit of an odd couple."

"Did we date?" he asked. "You called us a couple."

"No, I meant that in the most platonic way possible." She felt her smile slip.

"But you were friends with my wife," he said. "I'm just trying to piece it all together here."

"Before you two started dating, Mia hung out with us a lot, too, and she was crazy about you. She harbored this huge crush, and it took you a while to clue in."

Sawyer met her gaze, but didn't answer.

"So, maybe you had more options than I did," Olivia conceded. "But Mia was beautiful and fun, and she could ride better than you."

"I don't know why, but I feel mildly insulted with that," he said with a soft laugh. "How well do I ride?"

"Better than you play baseball," she joked. But then she remembered that he didn't know, and she sobered. "You're a really good rider. You always have been. You go on the cattle drives to move the herd, and you come back with all these stories about hungry wolves and belligerent cows." She paused, remembering the way his eyes would sparkle when he embellished his tales. "You taught me to ride."

"Am I a good teacher?" he asked.

"No." She crossed her arms, as if she needed to defend her position on that. But he really hadn't been. He expected his students to function on instinct, like he did.

"No?" He laughed softly. "But you said I taught you. That's something."

"You're bossy," she countered. "You yell a lot when you're teaching. After that first ride, I wouldn't take your calls for a week."

"Oh. Sorry. Obviously, we made up."

"Just barely." Olivia chuckled. "We had

fun, mostly. When you weren't bossing me around and telling me I'd get myself killed. We were good friends."

"So, this is your chance to turn the tables, I guess," he said, sobering. "I'm the one who doesn't know what he's doing."

"I'm a nicer teacher," she said with a short laugh. "You don't have to worry that I'll take my revenge."

The coffee maker burbled as it dribbled fresh brew into the pot, and Bella toddled up to her father and held a plastic toy up for his inspection. Sawyer bent down, looked at the toy seriously, then said, "Very nice. I like it."

Bella looked at the plastic block in her fingers as if seeing it again for the first time. Then she smiled up at Sawyer, her blue eyes glittering.

The girls remembered their father just fine, and they obviously recognized their daddy in this broken version of him. Olivia recognized the old Sawyer in him, too. She always had been able to get him to relax. But there was something different there, as well…something foreign around the edges. When you stripped away someone's memories, maybe it loosened up other parts of their personality that had been held down.

Or maybe there had been sides to him that she'd never known...that he'd never opened to her. That was possible, too.

But she *had* been his friend, even if she'd kept her distance in the last few years.

Olivia pulled her phone out of her jeans pocket and glanced down at the screen. No missed calls. That meant that despite all the messages she'd left for her brother, telling him she was going to be in Beaut, Brian hadn't called her. She'd come back to town for Brian...to try and mend this rift between them. If it weren't for him, she wouldn't have returned. Her life here was over—this town couldn't be home for her again.

"Sawyer, I'm going to go make a call," she said.

Sawyer looked up from where he crouched next to his daughters. "Sure."

Olivia slipped out the side door and walked

a few paces away from the house. She could hear the growl of a tractor's engine somewhere in the distance, and the sunlight warmed her shoulders. There was no breeze right now, just sunny warmth, and she dialed her brother's number once more.

It rang four times, then the voice mail kicked in: "Hi, it's Brian. You know what to do."

She hung up. She'd already left three messages.

Lord, what do I do? she prayed. *He won't talk to me, and I'm kind of intimidated here. He's my little brother, and he can't stand me. Do I deserve this?*

Olivia had said she was leaving Beaut in order to go to school, but there was more than a simple desire for an education and a career that pulled her away. This town was the kind of place that had a long memory. Olivia had always thought of herself as pretty tough, but those rumors had been devastating. People looked at her differently. They whispered when she walked by. It didn't matter that the rumors weren't true—they were juicy, so they had spread like wildfire. They had affected the way Olivia saw herself, eroding her sense of self-worth. Just as soon as she and her mother had scraped up enough money for college, she'd left for Montana State University and never looked back.

The problem was, she felt guilty. She'd had good reason to leave Beaut, but she'd left Brian behind, and she'd always been a little extra protective of him. From where Brian stood, Olivia had abandoned both him and their mom. They hadn't known she was sick yet, and when Olivia left town she'd thought she had decades left with her mother in her life. And now that she wanted to make up with her brother, he wasn't interested.

Still, Brian didn't know that she might have a solution to their mutual money problem…

As if on cue, her cell phone rang, and she looked down, hoping to see Brian's number.

It wasn't—it was the Whites. She sighed and picked up the call.

"Hello?"

"Olivia." It was Irene. "You must have arrived in Beaut by now."

"Yes, I'm here," she said. "I arrived this afternoon."

"Have you spoken with Sawyer yet? I mean, I hate to hound you, but Wyatt and I are just sitting here waiting, and the wait is worse than when Wyatt was running for office!" Irene laughed at her own little joke.

"Right." Olivia sighed. "Well, I'm going to need a bit of time. As you know, I haven't been back to town in years, and I cut a lot of ties when I left, so…"

"Will Sawyer not talk to you?" Irene asked.

"No, it isn't that, it's just… I appreciate that you're willing to help Brian and me with the hospital debt, and believe me, I don't want to jeopardize that. But I need to be able to do this in my own way."

"We don't mean to be demanding, but we

are offering you a rather large recompense for your time," Irene said.

"But it is *my time*," Olivia replied, then tried to soften her tone. "I want to help you reconcile with Sawyer—you know that. But this can't be rushed."

"We'd just like a general timeline, so we aren't jumping at every phone call," Irene said.

Was that a reasonable request? Probably, but the situation here in Beaut was not what any of them had anticipated, and Olivia suddenly felt tight-lipped about the details.

Sawyer was incredibly vulnerable right now, and he'd asked her to help him remember...not to complicate his life further with his late wife's parents. If they knew he didn't remember them, they might seize the moment to press him when he had no ammunition to fight back. She couldn't let that happen. When his memory returned, she could present their case, but until then, she couldn't take advantage of his weakness for her own gain—or for the Whites'.

"I'm not playing games. I don't know how long this will be, but I will call you the second I have news."

Irene sighed, then there was the muffled sound of her covering the phone and the murmur of voices. Then she came back on the line. "We appreciate anything you can do on our behalf, Olivia. You're like a daughter to us."

A daughter who had to do them favors to get one in return…but still. They'd kept Olivia close after Mia's passing, and in a way, it seemed to keep Mia's memory alive for all of them.

"I'll be in touch as soon as I can," Olivia said. "I promise."

After saying goodbye, she hung up the phone, and stared at it in her palm for a moment.

The Whites wanted results, and they were used to getting them. Wyatt White was a senator, and his wife had been the financial engine behind his political career. They were used to having to wait on results for things like elections, but not being forced to wait by people like Olivia.

She was putting off the very people who could lift the burden for her and Brian, but her conscience wouldn't allow her to do any less.

Father, guide me, she prayed. She needed God's blessing more than she needed the Whites' money.

Coffee had been something familiar— making it, waiting for it, listening to the sound of the burbling coffee maker... And Sawyer had so little that was familiar. Olivia said he used to like his coffee sweet and creamy, so he was giving it a try. He took a sip, and made a face. Too sweet, a bit filmy on his tongue.

The screen door clattered shut behind Olivia as she came back into the kitchen.

"Don't like it?" she asked. "Which one is that?"

"This is cream and sugar," he replied, and turned to dump the mugful of coffee down the drain. He poured a fresh mug and took a sip of the black coffee. It tasted fresh, bitter, smooth. "Mmm. Yeah. This is good."

Olivia pulled out her phone, glanced down at the screen, and then pocketed it again. She looked distracted, and he felt a wave of misgiving.

"Are you putting off plans for me?" Sawyer asked.

"Hmm?"

"You're checking your phone," he said. "If you have stuff to do, I don't want to keep you here. I know my uncle is worried about me, but I can handle the girls for a while—"

"No, no," she said quickly. "I'm fine. It's nothing."

He didn't believe that. He might not remember Olivia, but he knew what tension looked like, and she had tension written all over her. It was brought out by baseball and phone calls, apparently.

"I'm not as helpless as I look," he said, and he made a point of not touching the bandage on his head.

"I don't think you're helpless," she said.

"Sure, you do." He fixed her with a direct look. "And I might not have my memory, but I'm okay. I don't want to be your obligation here."

"Sawyer, you have a brain injury. You might have all the best of intentions, but you need a little looking after. Sorry to break it to you."

A faint smile tickled at the corners of her lips, and he thought he saw some friendly teasing in that gaze. Maybe it wasn't so terrible to be spending a few days with this woman. They'd been friends once, apparently, and he could tell what he must have seen in her before. She was likeable.

When she looked at him like that, he was reminded again of that fragment of memory—the woman in the black coat, how he had put his hand out to touch her. She turned…and he couldn't remember more than that. Except this time, he recalled snow on the ground—mucky, wet, dirty snow on the edge of a sidewalk. Nothing else. It was frustrating having these little shards of memory that didn't connect. He needed to find where they fit in.

And he had already tried doing that sitting inside.

"Okay, so even if I am recovering here, it doesn't mean we have to sit in the house and stare at each other. You want to get out for a bit? I have a feeling Lloyd is going to be a while."

"I have that same feeling," she agreed. "What did you have in mind?"

"Well, my uncle doesn't want me helping out on the ranch until my memory's back. So maybe we could start out where I used to work—at the barn maybe." He looked down at his rough, calloused hands. "You said I used to work a lot, right?"

"You did," she agreed. "It might jog a few memories."

Bella and Lizzie looked up at them, and Olivia glanced around the kitchen. "We should bring something for the girls. What do they snack on?"

"Um…" Yeah, and he'd just been saying he could take care of things on his own. "I'm not sure."

Olivia opened a cupboard, looked through the contents and then moved on to the next.

"Yesterday they each had a sippy cup around this time of day. Lloyd got it for them," he added.

Olivia went to the fridge and opened it. "Ta-da." She pulled out two cups, both filled with milk. The toddlers beelined toward her, holding their hands out for the milk, and she gave them the cups. The girls started to drink. Bella spun in a circle as she slurped on the rubber mouthpiece, and Lizzie sat down to drink.

"Cereal?" Sawyer asked, pulling a box of Cheerios out of a bottom cupboard.

"Put some into a baggie," Olivia said.

"I don't know where to find those…"

The next few minutes were spent putting a toddler-friendly snack together and piling everything into a diaper bag that Sawyer did know the location of. It turned out that there weren't baggies, but there were plastic containers, and soon enough they were heading out the side door, each of them carrying a child in their arms, and the diaper bag slung over Sawyer's shoulder. He glanced back at Olivia, and shot her a smile. It felt good having her here with him—a little less lonely. Or was he just responding to being with a beautiful woman? Here's hoping he wasn't that shallow.

They headed down the gravel drive toward a winding road. It was downhill from there toward the barn—Sawyer had stared at it all morning, trying to tease some memories free. A young blue jay squawked at them from high in a tree.

"Birdie," Bella said.

"Yeah, that's right." He smiled down at his daughter, then glanced over at Olivia. "So, tell me about you and me. What should I remember?"

"You're older than me by about two years, so we didn't run in the same circles," she said. "But you liked to eat in the diner where

I was working, and one night you were the only guy in there. And we started talking. Turned out, we both liked the same movies."

"And rest is history?" he said wryly.

"I guess so. We got along. I mean, we didn't have a lot in common. You were a ranch hand, and I was a recent high school grad, saving up to go to college for nursing. You were ready to spend the rest of your life here while I was pretty determined to get out of town. Your girlfriend had already graduated a year before, and after she worked for a year, she left for college. I think she was going to travel a bit first. Anyway, before she left, she dumped you. That was at the same time I was graduating. So when we met, you were a bit heartbroken."

"Ouch…" he murmured, but he didn't feel it. It just seemed like the appropriate thing to say. This was like listening to a story about other people. He couldn't remember any of it.

"We just…clicked," she said. "We cheered each other up."

"So, what did we do together?" he asked.

"Oh, we went to movies, ate out, went to the local fair…that kind of thing. I was your date at some family event, but that was just because your great aunt had been overly attached to your ex-girlfriend, so you needed some distraction." She laughed softly. "She wasn't overly attached to *me*…"

"So I have a great aunt?" he asked.

"You did. She passed away, I think."

Their boots crunched over the gravel, and Bella started to wriggle in his arms, so he set her down and let her walk. Olivia followed his lead and put Lizzie down, too.

"And you came back to see me…" He looked over at her, and some color tinted Olivia's cheeks.

"I came back for my own reasons. Seeing you was…a bonus."

"Ah." Sawyer pushed his hands into his pockets. "You aren't going to tell me, are you?"

"Tell you what?" Her gaze flickered toward him.

"What was really between us," he said.

Olivia sighed. "I'm being honest. We were friends. All friendships have different balances between them, I suppose."

"And ours?" he prodded.

"Like I said, your girlfriend left you for college," she said. "And I was going to do the same thing. I had plans to get my education and I didn't want a life here in Beaut. We both knew that a romantic relationship between us couldn't go anywhere."

"So there was some history between us... something more than just friendship," he clarified.

"You ended up marrying my best friend," she replied. "That's the history that matters."

"I agree, but you and I stayed in touch, it seems."

"I came to the wedding," Olivia replied. "I was the maid of honor. But after that, I... gave you two space."

"So, we didn't manage to hold on to that friendship after all," he said. Why was she being evasive here? He could sense that there was something more she didn't want to tell him.

"No," she said.

He nodded. Apparently, he'd had his own life with his wife. It seemed strange that they'd just lose touch like that, and a little sad they'd lost a friendship that had mattered to them very much. What wasn't she telling him? "So, why did you come back? Why did you show up here?"

"Because—" Olivia cast him an apologetic look. "I came back to see my brother. I have to patch things together with him one way or another, and he's really bitter toward me. I'd hoped that you might be able to help me with that...but obviously, you have your own stuff to deal with right now."

They both paused as the toddlers got distracted with a stick. She wasn't here for him, exactly. That might explain the tension he sensed in her earlier.

"Maybe I can still help," he offered.

"No." Her voice firmed. "You need to get

your memory back. Don't worry about me. I'll sort it out."

"I guess I'm not much use right now," he admitted.

"Not for this," she said. "Just focus on getting better."

The barn wasn't far away now, and Sawyer's gaze swept across the cow-dotted field, over the corral that held a couple of horses. Was this familiar? He dug about inside his head, looking for something, some sense of connection at the very least...but there was nothing.

"Horsey!" Lizzie said, pointing. She hopped up and down. "Daddy! Horsey!"

"She must like horses," Olivia said. "Should we take them over to get a closer look?"

"Yeah, sure."

But his mind wasn't on his daughter's delight. He was wondering why he felt some strange sense of connectedness with Olivia, and had felt nothing when Lloyd had shown him pictures of his dead wife. What did that say about him? Had Sawyer been a good husband? Had he harbored feelings for another woman? He didn't like that thought. He might not remember anything, but he did have a sense of right and wrong.

Who was I?

And would he be proud of who he was once he figured that out?

They headed down a straight road that led to the barn. There were no workers around that Sawyer could see, and the lowing of cattle that came on the grass-scented breeze was oddly soothing to his system. He sucked in a deep breath, feeling the muscles in his shoulders relax.

Bella came over to Sawyer and held up her hands. He picked her up and she settled against his shoulder, one tiny hand planted on the back of his neck. Lizzie came running up, too, but Olivia swept her up into her arms and made an exaggerated surprised face.

"What happened there?" Olivia asked Lizzie. "Did I get you?"

Lizzie laughed, and Sawyer couldn't help

but smile. He'd known these toddlers for all of two days that he could remember, but he was already attached. Sawyer led the way over to the corral.

The largest of the two horses ambled over toward them, pushing his nose into Sawyer's chest, snuffling against his pocket.

"I didn't think to bring a treat," he said, glancing over his shoulder at Olivia.

"All we have in the bag is Cheerios and cheese cubes," Olivia said with a low laugh.

"Horsey…" Bella breathed, and then she put a hand on the horse's long nose.

The horse pulled back, shaking his head, and moved over toward Olivia. She took a step back.

"Sorry, buddy," she said.

The horse ambled off again, and Sawyer felt all of his own tension seeping away. Bella clearly loved horses, but it looked like he did, too. There was something about those rippling muscles, the shining coats, the smell of dust and sweat and the tang of manure…

"Num-nums," Lizzie said, patting Olivia's shoulder. "Num-nums."

"I think she wants her snack."

Sawyer passed her the diaper bag, and she squatted down, put Lizzie on the ground and opened the bag. Lizzie looked into the depth and pulled out a plastic container of cheese cubes. Olivia opened it for her and she reached in and came out with a single cube between two chubby fingers.

"Mmm. That looks good," Olivia murmured.

"Num-nums!" Bella said, launching herself downward.

"Whoa!" Her motion caught Sawyer by surprise, and he almost dropped the girl before he was able to get a grip on her wriggling body. He managed to deposit her on the ground right side up. Bella headed straight for the cheese cubes. Such trust—the kid hadn't even paused to appreciate that she hadn't landed on her head.

Olivia held the container out toward Bella. Sawyer was glad that Olivia was here to think of things like snacks. Maybe he needed more help around here than he thought.

"Lizzie?" Olivia stood up, and Sawyer looked around, scanning for the girl. She was gone...and both of their gazes swung toward the corral.

Somehow, the toddler slipped away in those few heartbeats when her sister had the attention, and little Lizzie with her ruffled curls and little pink running shoes stood in the center of the corral, her face tipped upward in rapture as she stared up at the massive stallion.

Sawyer's heart thudded to a stop.

Chapter Three

Olivia shot out a hand out, grabbing Bella by the arm before she could follow her sister. How had Olivia done that—completely missed Lizzie disappearing? Tears of panic rose in her eyes.

Lizzie stood next to the irritable stallion, and it was like time slowed to a crawl and Olivia could see every single, painstaking detail as the toddler reached her hand out toward the stallion's leg. He lifted his hoof and brought it down in a sharp stamp, dust billowing up from the ground around his hoof.

Olivia pulled Bella up into her arms and

had taken a step toward the corral when Sawyer's iron grip caught her by the shoulder.

"No," he snapped. "Stay here."

His tone was so authoritative that she stopped in her tracks, watching as he ducked down under a rail, easing his body through. Sawyer straightened to his full height and walked slowly toward his daughter.

The stallion snorted and pawed the ground, eyeing Sawyer with an irritable glint in his eye. Lizzie reached out and touched the stallion's knee, and in response, the big animal reared up, hooves pawing the air.

Sawyer dashed in, caught Lizzie up in one arm, and put a protective hand up as the stallion came back down again.

"Whoa…" Sawyer intoned. "Whoa now… Hey…."

The stallion made another couple of little jumps with his front hooves, but didn't rear again. Sawyer stayed facing the horse and backed slowly toward the fence again. When he got there, he handed Lizzie over the rails into Olivia's arms, then ducked down and eased himself through.

Olivia held both girls tightly, her heart hammering in her chest.

"That was close—" she breathed.

"Yeah—a little too close," Sawyer said, glancing over his shoulder toward the stallion once more. "That horse is in a mood. I doubt he's even ridable."

He sounded like himself again—knowledgeable, confident.

"I wouldn't know," she said. "But you did. Sawyer, you knew what to do!"

Sawyer's gaze flipped toward her, and he smiled weakly. "I did. You're right. I knew what to do. I knew the signs. I know what an angry horse looks like…"

"Do you remember anything else?" she asked hopefully.

Sawyer licked his lips, glanced back toward the corral. Then he sighed and took Lizzie from her arms.

"Nah. I'm trying. I don't know why I knew what to do, I just—"

"You reacted," she said.

"I guess." He started toward the road, and Olivia grabbed the diaper bag and caught up to him. He was a tall man, and she almost had to jog to keep up.

"Sawyer, slow down," she said with a low laugh.

"Sorry." He cast her a rueful smile.

"Horsey!" Lizzie said, leaning her entire body toward the corral.

"Yeah, that's enough of that," Sawyer said. They walked together in silence for a few paces, and Olivia eyed Sawyer.

"I'm sorry," she said. "I was the one who had Lizzie, and I got distracted for a minute there—"

"It's okay." Sawyer glanced down at her, those dark eyes catching her gaze and holding it. "I guess we just found out how fast these kids are."

"I guess," she agreed. "I'm new to this, too."

"Not a bad thing to know." Sawyer looked

down at Lizzie grimly. "Fast and cute. I'm in trouble."

Olivia was tempted to laugh, but Sawyer's solemn expression hadn't changed a bit.

"My heart nearly stopped," Sawyer said, turning toward Olivia. "When I saw her in there next to that horse, I thought I was going to throw up. I mean, like more than just regular panic when a kid's not where she should be..."

"Like a dad," Olivia said softly.

"Is that what it's like to be a father?" he asked.

"I think so," she said. A memory of her own dad rose in her mind—foggy, maybe even mostly made up at this point. She had a couple of pictures of her father, but he'd left them when she was eight and her brother wasn't much older than the toddlers were.

"I feel really bad that I don't know my daughters," Sawyer went on. "What kind of a dad forgets his kids?"

"This accident wasn't your fault," she countered. At least with Sawyer it had been an accident. Her father had just walked out—done with all of them, apparently.

"I know, but—" His shoulders lifted in a shrug. "I don't remember how I felt when they were born, but I do know how I felt when I saw Lizzie in that corral. I don't think I've forgotten everything."

The toddlers both began to squirm, and they put them down to let them run ahead. Sawyer was somber.

"Are you okay?" Olivia asked after some silence.

"Was I a good man?" he asked, and the question seemed to come out of the blue. She eyed him for a moment.

"Of course!" She started to smile, but then saw the seriousness in his gaze. "Sawyer, you were an upright guy. You worked hard and loved hard. You were honest. You were a real salt-of-the-earth type."

"Thing is, I don't remember my wife," he said. "At least I don't think so. I remember a black coat. Did she have a black coat?"

"I don't know," Olivia said. "But honestly,

Sawyer. You don't seem to remember much of anyone. Don't be so hard on yourself."

"When I saw you, I didn't know you, but you felt...familiar. Like with my instincts with Lizzie just now, I sensed that you were someone who mattered to me."

"Isn't that good to have it start to come back?" she asked tentatively.

"Did *you* have a black coat?" he asked.

"Maybe?" She eyed him uncertainly. "Why?"

"I think I remember a woman in a coat. Whatever. It's not much more than that. It could be anyone. But I've looked at my wedding album," Sawyer said. "I've held the wedding rings in my hand. I looked at the engagement ring I bought for her...and nothing. I didn't feel a thing."

"Did you feel anything when you saw my picture?" she asked.

He hesitated. "No."

"Maybe it's just that—I'm a real person. A picture is different."

Olivia put a hand on his arm and they

slowed to a stop. The girls stopped ahead to investigate some buttercups at the side of the road.

"Sawyer, you were a good guy," she said firmly. "And you loved each other. Mia knew you inside and out, and she trusted you."

"Then why did you back off?" he asked pointedly. "You'd think we could have emailed, kept up on social media...something."

Why did he keep picking at this? Why did he want to know every uncomfortable detail about their friendship? In some ways, they had been too close. In other ways, they'd never opened up enough. It had been a painful balancing act toward the end, and it was a relief when Mia had gone all moon-eyed over him, because Mia had been willing to throw herself into a relationship with Sawyer. That was the way these things were supposed to work—fall for each other, and then go for it! When it came to Sawyer and Olivia, they'd fallen for each other, and then held back.

"I was leaving town. I hated this place, Sawyer! What do you want me to say? I couldn't make my life here—I needed the city, where no one knew me so I could figure out who I was from scratch. This town is gossipy and can be downright cruel. I was ready to shake the dust off my boots and get out of here. Beaut couldn't be my home. You knew that. Besides, you had Mia. So maybe that was a bit painful for me."

Sawyer paused. She'd said too much already.

"Why was that painful?"

"I backed off after your wedding because you told me to," she said, tears misting her eyes, and she remembered what it felt like to have Sawyer look her in the eye and ask her to go away for a while. It had hurt—it had felt a whole lot like betrayal. But she'd understood, too. "You asked me to give you space, and I did."

Sawyer nodded. "The thing is, I don't think I would have asked you to back off unless my feelings for you were a threat to my marriage."

There it was—his worry. He was wondering if he was the kind of guy to be emotionally unfaithful to his wife. Well, she could set him straight there.

"Feelings—what do they matter?" Olivia demanded. "They come and they go. A vow—that matters! You chose the right woman, and every choice after that was in defense of your marriage. Those choices matter. You weren't untrue to her. The fact that you guarded your marriage means it was worth guarding, not that I was any threat. I promise you that."

"You sure?" he asked quietly.

"Positive. I'm not that kind of woman, either. Trust me." She'd been Mia's best friend, after all. And just because she'd backed away from Sawyer didn't mean that her friendship with Mia had been over. "Mia had your heart, and was confident in that. You were not in love with me. Maybe I was a little too close, but it wasn't more than that. She would have cut me off if it were. Trust me. She guarded those boundaries, too."

Sawyer was quiet. "Good."

"You were faithful, Sawyer. In every way. You were in love with Mia. You'll remember that soon enough. I know it."

"So why don't I remember her?" he asked. "If she was the woman I was in love with—"

"Maybe because it was easy with her," Olivia replied. "She didn't fight with you like I did. Maybe you remember more of me because I made you so mad."

"I thought we got along," he said.

"We did…but I could still drive you nuts." She shot him a grin. "Like no other."

Most of all, she'd driven him crazy because she couldn't be what he'd wanted. Not even if she'd tried to be. Olivia believed in God working all things together for good. She'd come to Beaut to help her own family on this trip, but maybe God had sent her to help Sawyer, too. In some mysterious way. She'd never been the wife for Sawyer, but maybe she could help him to remember the good guy he'd been. He deserved that.

That night, after the twins were asleep and the disconcertingly pretty Olivia had gone to bed, Sawyer sat in the kitchen, his elbows resting on the table. He couldn't sleep. It was possible that he'd had coffee too late in the day. Was that a problem for him normally? He had no idea.

The only sound was the hum of the refrigerator and the soft tick of a clock behind him on the wall.

I'm scared. I don't know who I am.

Sawyer sent the thought out there into the unknown, and he felt a little better, somehow, for having done it.

He wasn't sure who he was talking to, but it felt familiar, putting his feelings into words...into a plea. Having his head empty of memories was a strange burden. He was flapping in the wind with nothing to nail him down. He remembered a few odd things—like that marker, or how to make coffee, or how to deal with an angry horse. He wasn't completely helpless, exactly, but he had no people in his head, no connections beyond what he'd formed over the last couple of days. He desperately wished he could remember Mia, because while losing his wife must have been a horrible blow, the loneliness of forgetting her was deafening.

Sawyer heard boots on the step. The side door opened and Lloyd came in. The older man was dusty, and one pant leg was coated in half-dried mud. He pulled off his trucker hat and tossed it onto a peg. Without the hat, Lloyd looked softer, somehow. And a little goofier. That beaten-up hat seemed to give the man credibility.

"Fourteen new calves," Lloyd announced.

"Yeah?" Sawyer cast about in his brain, looking for an appropriate reply. This used to be his work. This used to be second nature to him.

"Do you remember what that means?" Lloyd asked. "It's the spring calve."

Sawyer shrugged. "Sorry. Wish I was

more help. I assume that's a good thing—the calves."

Maybe if Sawyer was tossed into a calving emergency, something would come back.

"Yeah, it's a good thing." Lloyd cast him an indulgent smile. "There'll be more tonight, too. And tomorrow. So far so good. No complications. The ranch hands are working hard...not that I'm trying to make you feel bad."

"I could come out with you," Sawyer offered.

"Nah. Not yet. I can't be keeping you out of trouble while doing my own work. Don't worry about it. You just rest up and get better. How's the head feeling?"

Sawyer reached up and touched the bandage. "It's still bruised. It doesn't ache like before, though."

"That's something," Lloyd said. "You shoulda seen you drop. I thought you'd cracked a bone in that thick skull of yours."

Sawyer chuckled. "I remembered something today. Sort of."

"Yeah?" Lloyd stopped, fixing him with a hopeful look.

"Olivia and I went out with the girls. Lizzie got into the corral, and I knew what to do. This big, angry stallion was rearing, and I was able to get her out of there. I just...knew what to do."

"That's excellent." His uncle grinned. "Do you remember the chores? What to do in the barn?"

"I—" Sawyer tried to think, push through the dark fog. "Maybe I would if I was faced with them. I don't know... I mean—"

"It's okay. It hasn't been that long since the accident." Lloyd shook his head.

"I figured out which kid was which," Sawyer added.

"You remembered?" Lloyd asked. "The doctor said that when it starts to come back, it might happen fast—"

"Not exactly," Sawyer admitted. "We... got them to say their names. And then I wrote their initials in permanent marker on their hands."

"Olivia didn't stop you?" Lloyd asked with a low laugh.

"Nope."

"Well… I guess we'll be clear on who's who, then." Lloyd shook his head. "That's like you, though. Pragmatic. It'll wash off eventually."

"Yeah, but for now, I need it. Their father should at least know them apart, right?"

Lloyd looked at him thoughtfully for a moment. "It'll come back, you know. The doctors both said you'll remember again."

"I know," he replied.

"So, this won't be forever, this…this…purgatory you're living in." Lloyd squinted at him.

"Sure hope not," Sawyer said. "I don't like not knowing who I am."

"You're still you," Lloyd countered. "You're still my nephew, whether you remember all the years we worked together or not. You're family—that's just a fact."

Like his girls—they were still his. His memories didn't cement them to him…not fully, at least. There was something deeper that connected them. Blood. Or a wedding vow. Olivia had said that counted for more than feelings, and maybe she was right.

"I appreciate it," Sawyer said, and when he looked up at the older man, he saw tears glistening in his eyes.

Lloyd cleared his throat and blinked back the emotion. "I'll get you out working with me again, even if I have to teach you from scratch."

"I could start now," Sawyer said. "If I'm beginning to remember a couple of things, it might help."

"After calving," Lloyd said. "When it slows down a bit. Then I'll show you the ropes. Once the doctor gives you the all clear. If you toppled over out there—"

"I'm not going to topple over," Sawyer retorted.

"Didn't think you'd get kicked in the head the first time," Lloyd said. "That happens again, and you might be dead. So no, not yet. After calving."

Sawyer nodded. The thought of getting out there and learning to be useful again was appealing. Maybe by then, he wouldn't have to be taught from scratch anymore, and he'd remember his job.

"Say, if I drink coffee too late in the day, does it keep me awake?" Sawyer asked.

"Yup." Lloyd glanced toward the pot. "You never drink it after noon."

"Good to know," he said, then smiled wryly. "I guess I'll be up for a while."

Lloyd peeled off his boots, then headed for the kitchen sink. He turned on the tap and squirted some dish soap into his hands.

"Olivia said I used to drink my coffee with cream and sugar," he added.

"You used to. That was a while ago. Then your doctor warned you about all that sugar, and you went cold turkey and learned to like it black. Why...you going back to the old way?"

"No, I still like it black," he said.

Lloyd finished washing his hands and

turned toward him. "See? It's all in there. Just a matter of getting it back again."

"Yup." That's what Olivia kept saying, too. They seemed to recognize him still, even if he couldn't recognize himself.

"You used to sit up in the kitchen reading your Bible," Lloyd went on. "It was your way to unwind and get your mind settled to sleep. You'd drink some warm milk and read a passage or two."

Sawyer raised an eyebrow. "Yeah?"

"You know, if you wanted to go through some motions and see if it helped kick-start anything."

"Thanks. I might try that."

"You're a Christian, Sawyer."

"Huh." He sucked in a breath. "I didn't know that."

"Hold on." Lloyd headed out of the kitchen, leaving Sawyer alone. He returned a moment later with a worn, black Bible in one hand. He deposited it on the kitchen table.

Sawyer opened the Bible randomly and

saw some blue pen underlines. He flipped another few pages and found more.

"This is mine?"

"Yup."

Sawyer flipped to the front, and he saw his name printed on the dedication page. Underneath was written, *From your dad.*

"My dad gave it to me," he murmured, and he had a flash of something in his memory... an aroma—a mixture of Old Spice cologne and hay. It was a little musky. But he couldn't recall a face.

"You remembering something?" Lloyd asked.

"I don't know. Almost. It's close."

"Your old man gave you that Bible when you were a teenager. He died before your senior year and you came to live here with me."

"Oh..." Sawyer nodded a couple of times, sadness oozing up inside of him. Funny to grieve for a man he couldn't remember, but that scent was in his head now, and it was probably the smell he associated with his dad. It was a start.

"He'd be glad to know you've still got that Bible," Lloyd said. "He was a man of faith."

Sawyer leafed through the pages again, and he touched a place where there was some underlining in blue pen.

"You underlined the passages that meant something to you," Lloyd said.

"I guess they wouldn't mean much to me now," he said quietly.

"Says who?" Lloyd retorted. "That's the thing with the Good Book. You read something once and it speaks to your heart. Then you read it again a few years later, and you don't remember what it meant to you back then, but it suddenly means something a bit different. I almost envy you tonight."

"Why's that?" Sawyer asked.

"Because you get to read those passages again for the first time."

Sawyer looked down at the worn pages. Some had torn and had been taped back together again. He thumbed through some pages, and the Bible naturally opened toward the middle, in the book of Psalms. He

smoothed a hand over the words, his calloused fingers making a whispering noise
against the rice-paper-thin pages. He didn't
remember how to pray, either, but he knew
the concept of it.

I'm scared. I don't know who I am.

And this time, he knew Who he was di-
recting those words toward in his heart.

"Where should I start—" he began to ask,
lifting his head. But Lloyd had left the room.
Sawyer was alone again, but he didn't feel
quite so isolated this time. The Bible was
open on the table in front of him. His gaze
fell to Psalm 121.

The Lord is thy keeper: the Lord is thy
shade upon thy right hand.

The sun shall not smite thee by day,
nor the moon by night.

The Lord shall preserve thee from all
evil: he shall preserve thy soul.

The Lord shall preserve thy going out
and thy coming in from this time forth,
and even for evermore.

"From this time forth, and even for evermore," Sawyer murmured.

Whatever was in the past was gone so completely that he couldn't even remember it. But if God would guide his steps from now on...if Sawyer could face this strange, confusing, memory-less world with God at his side, maybe he could find his footing, after all.

Lord, I don't remember what You've done for me. I don't remember what I've done wrong, or right. I don't even know if I'm a good man. I have this nagging feeling that I wasn't as good as I should have been, and I can't let that rest. I just know that I'm adrift and alone, and I'm scared. Lloyd said I was a Christian. And I want to continue being one. If You'll take me.

Sawyer felt a warmth around him, and his fears seemed to drift away. In the here and now, he was not alone, and he had a feeling that he never had been. He used to know God, and even if his memories were gone, there was a part of him that had kept on praying out into the void. He flipped the pages of his Bible again, and his gaze stopped at another passage that had been underlined, re-underlined, and even highlighted.

The Lord is my shepherd; I shall not want.

And with those words, his first memory came flooding back. He was in a drafty room with other children, and a lady was sitting in front of them in a modest dress, her knees pressed together. She had thick glasses and a sweet smile.

"Let's say it all together," she'd intoned. "'The Lord is my shepherd; I shall not want...'"

And they'd all recited the words together, monotone and flat in the way kids did when they'd memorized something.

"'He maketh me to lie down in green pastures...' Mrs. Willoughby," Sawyer said aloud, and tears pricked at his eyes.

He remembered her! She was kind and

smelled like peppermints. She'd always had tissues on hand because she suffered from hay fever, and she sneezed a lot. He cast about, feeling for more memories that were connected to this one, but he couldn't land on anything. Just the image of that Sunday school teacher sitting in front of the class, a tissue clasped in one hand, as she helped them recite the Twenty-Third Psalm.

But it was something more than a frustrating fragment about a black coat he couldn't quite place—he had one solid memory!

Chapter Four

The next morning was Sunday, and Olivia blinked her eyes open to a ray of sunlight that had landed on her pillow. She rubbed her eyes and reached for her cell phone to check the time. It was seven—sleeping in by a ranch's standards. She lay under the warm quilt for a moment longer, yesterday's events coming back to mind. She'd come to Beaut to help the Whites reconnect with Sawyer, but it wouldn't be as easy as she'd hoped.

It shouldn't be about money. Olivia wasn't a materialistic person, but a chance to reduce this pile of debt couldn't be ignored. It would be nothing for the White family to call in a few favors.

The White family had moved out to Beaut in order to start Wyatt's political run— giving him connections to some powerful local ranchers. Sending their daughter to the local public school had been a public relations choice, meant to make their family look down-to-earth. Mia had told Olivia that much in confidence. Wyatt White had gone about "pressing flesh" and listening to the concerns of the average Joe. But the Whites had never worried like the average Joe had to worry when it came to money.

They didn't worry about bills, but they had worried about Mia. Wyatt and Irene had some glorious plans for their much-loved only child that hadn't included marrying a common ranch hand. But Mia had loved Sawyer, and if there was one thing Mia'd learned from "roughing it" out here in rural Montana, it was that she wasn't any better than anyone else. And that common ranch hand had been quite good enough for Mia White.

Olivia tossed back her quilt and reached for her clothes. The room was chilly this time of the morning, and she could hear the soothing murmur of voices from the kitchen.

It wasn't easy watching Sawyer fall for Mia, but Olivia hadn't been the right one for him. It didn't matter that they'd harbored feelings for each other ever since that night in the diner, or that they'd clicked in a way that Olivia hadn't experienced before or since. Sawyer needed a woman who wanted to make her life in Beaut, and Mia was willing to give up everything her family connections offered her for this man.

So when Olivia said that Mia deserved him, she meant it. Because with the rumors swirling around town about Olivia sleeping with all those guys, with the sidelong looks, the crude jokes, the name-calling, the bullying…she couldn't stay.

Olivia pulled on a pair of jeans and a sweatshirt, then went to the bathroom to brush her teeth and wash her face. As she was coming out of the bathroom, she heard some babbling coming from the toddlers' room down the hall. She paused, listening. No one else seemed to have noticed, so she headed in the direction of the children's laughter.

Pushing the door open, she found the girls, each standing up in her own crib. The room was still dark, the curtains pulled. So Olivia opened the curtains and the girls blinked up at her with smiles on their chubby faces.

"Good morning," she said, reaching down to pick up the first little girl. She had a *B* on her hand—so this one was Bella. "You ready for a new diaper?"

Olivia had learned the day before that keeping one toddler in a crib while she changed the other was the smartest move. So she grabbed a diaper and headed for the changing table on the opposite side of the room. The job was completed quickly enough, and just as Olivia was picking Bella up again from the changing table, the bedroom door opened, and Sawyer came inside.

"Hi," Olivia said with a smile. She passed Bella over to her father's arms. "She needs to get dressed. I'll do Lizzie's diaper."

"Sounds good. Thanks." Sawyer hoisted his daughter higher and headed for the dresser. "It's church today. Do you normally go?"

Olivia shrugged. "In the city, I go every week. Do *you*?"

"Why do you ask it like that?" He glanced over at her.

"Because when I knew you, you hated church. I mean, you believed in God, but—"

"But?" He raised an eyebrow.

"You were the kind of guy who loved to point out ugly church history and TV preachers who stole money and that kind of thing. You weren't much of a churchgoer."

"Oh..." He frowned slightly. "I thought I'd go this week, all the same."

Olivia held out her arms for Lizzie, who let out a squeal of happiness as Olivia lifted her out of the crib. "Okay..."

"You want to come with me?"

Olivia brought Lizzie to the changing table and reached for a diaper. "Sure. It might be nice to see some people I haven't talked with in a few years."

It wasn't the church people who had spread the nasty rumors about her in her senior year. Back then there weren't too many young people who attended regularly, anyway.

"My uncle said I was a Christian, and that sounded right to me, somehow. He didn't mention me being all bitter about church or anything."

Olivia shrugged. "Keep in mind, I didn't know you as well after you got married, so things might have changed. Mia loved being involved with church, and you loved Mia, so..."

He frowned, as if considering that for a moment. "I remembered someone last night."

Some*one*, not some*thing*.

"Did you?" Olivia looked over at him hopefully. Was it coming back now? Sawyer held Bella in one arm and was attempting to get a dress over her head with the other. "Who?"

"Mrs. Willoughby. My Sunday school teacher from when I was little." He stopped the slow-motion wrestle with his daughter.

"Anything about her specifically?" Olivia asked.

"Just her teaching us a Bible passage. Nothing more. Nothing else connected, just…that."

Sawyer managed to get the dress over Bella's head this time around, and he let out a chuckle of victory.

"Mom kept trying to get my brother to go to church, too," she said.

"He isn't a Christian?"

She shook her head. "He hasn't stepped foot in a church since Mom stopped forcing him as a kid."

"How long since you've seen him?" Sawyer asked.

"I came back to take care of my mom for a few weeks before she died five years ago. That was the spring before your wedding. By the time she found out she was sick, the cancer was really advanced, and there wasn't much time left. After my brother and I scattered her ashes, I went back to Billings. I wanted my brother to come with me, but he wouldn't. He said there was no point. A job in the city or a job in Beaut—it was all the same to him. He'd wanted to start his own mechanic shop, but there wasn't any money for that, and the hospital debt really did a number on both of our credit scores when we missed some payments. And there I was with my nursing job and my education…he was just mad, I guess. At everything. He'd just lost his mother too. I figured some time would heal the wounds. It hasn't so far."

"So you haven't seen him since then?" Sawyer clarified.

"No. Not since then. I tried making plans to have Christmas together, stuff like that, but he didn't want to. He always used the excuse that he was working, but I knew it wasn't that. Every time we talked, he was a little bit angrier. And I got defensive… I mean, it wasn't my fault! When I went off to college, we weren't planning on Mom getting sick. It wasn't fair to blame everything on me, as if I could control it. But maybe that was part of his grieving. I don't know."

Sawyer finished with Bella's dress and then reached for Lizzie. He grabbed a matching pink dress and began a balancing act with the second toddler.

"Was I around?" Sawyer asked.

"When Mom died?" Olivia asked.

"Yeah. We were friends, you said. Was I there to lend a hand at all?"

"It was the spring before your wedding," Olivia explained. "You and Mia were busy with your own stuff, but you guys helped out as much as I'd let you."

"That's good…" He looked up at her, and his eyes widened in sudden recognition. "The black coat…"

"What about it?" Olivia came over and helped to navigate Lizzie's grabbing hands into the armholes of the little dress.

"It's been bothering me," he said. "At first I could just remember the coat, and then I remembered it was on a mucky, snowy day. It was cold and wet. I was standing on a side-walk, I think. And there was this woman standing ahead of me in a black coat. I put my hand on her shoulder, and she turned back, and..."

Olivia's heart skipped a beat. She remembered it, too, now—standing on that sidewalk with the slushy snow coming down.

"...it was you," Sawyer said. "But you'd been crying. And..."

"And?" she whispered.

"I remember it now. I wanted to hug you. To try and make you feel better. I don't remember the context, though."

Olivia nodded sadly. "I do remember that. You saw me in town, and I hadn't told you yet that Mom had passed, although you knew it would happen soon. I hadn't told anyone. Brian might have... I don't know. I was in a bit of a fog."

It was a few years ago now, but remembering those aching, heartbroken days was still difficult.

"Did I hug you?" he asked uncertainly.

"No." She licked her lips. She knew exactly why she hadn't let him hug her. He'd moved toward her, and she'd pulled back. They'd agreed not to touch each other anymore—no more hugs, or nudges. It hadn't been appropriate, and while a death in the family might be an understandable excuse to lift the ban, she hadn't wanted to.

"Oh…" Sawyer nodded. "Look, I know this is going to sound a bit weird, but could I hug you now?"

Olivia blinked up at him, surprised.

"It was a while ago, Sawyer," she said, forcing what she hoped was a natural-sounding laugh. She tugged Lizzie's dress down. "I'm okay now. You don't have to worry about me."

"I know, but I don't have many memories rattling around in my head, and that's one of them. It's kind of uncomfortable—disjointed, lonely. If I could hug you now, it might make me feel better." Sawyer put Lizzie down on the floor with her sister, and then looked up at Olivia, those dark eyes meeting hers almost pleadingly.

"Oh..." Olivia shrugged. If it was for him, and not for her... "I guess that would be okay."

Sawyer looked down at her uncertainly for a moment. She met his gaze, wondering if maybe he'd change his mind, but then he slipped his arms around her. It was a soft hug, tender and careful. She leaned her cheek against his shoulder and laid her hands on his upper arms. He was stronger and more muscular than she'd realized, and she inhaled the musky scent of him. His arms were warm and his touch was gentle, pressing her against that broad chest of his where his heart thumped strong and slow. She felt him exhale slowly, and he rested his cheek against her hair.

It was such an unexpectedly tender moment that she felt tears mist her eyes. Maybe she should have let him hug her back then when she needed it most, except now she could clearly remember why she'd refused to let him pull her into his arms. It was because of this—the safety, the comfort, the longing that rose up inside of her at his touch. It was because these gentle arms had been too easy to fall into, and he'd been engaged to another woman. But that didn't mean she hadn't felt anything for him, and a hug like this one would have opened the emotional floodgates—the very last thing she needed on a slushy sidewalk in downtown Beaut.

Sawyer released her, and Olivia stepped back. She let out a shaky little sigh. The toddlers had opened a dresser drawer and were pulling out items of clothing, one at a time.

"Better?" she asked, forcing a smile.

"Yeah. I think so." He met her gaze, a smile turning up the corners of his lips. "That's the first hug of my life that didn't come from one of my daughters, as far as I can remember."

"That isn't the first adult hug of your life," she said, shaking her head. She personally remembered several—the kind that had woken up a part of her that she knew was best left dormant.

"It is today." His voice was low and warm.

"Okay. I'll give you that."

Sawyer shot her a grin, then headed over to the girls and picked up a little shirt, folded it neatly and replaced it in the drawer. As soon as it went inside, Lizzie grabbed it back out, and Bella let out a tinkle of laughter. Sawyer picked up the entire pile and dumped it unfolded into the drawer, then scooped up the girls, one in each arm. He pushed the drawer shut with his foot and turned back toward Olivia.

"We should eat," he said.

"Yes, we should."

That hug had left a warm feeling around her—the kind that could tip an entire day. Sawyer couldn't remember why they'd stopped hugging each other, but she did. There were some things that were best saved for romance—like the kinds of hugs that melted all of Olivia's carefully constructed walls.

When Sawyer had Mia, those no-touching rules in their relationship were a whole lot easier to manage. But Mia was gone now, and Olivia and Sawyer were both single. She'd never told him what his gentle squeezes did to her heart, and she'd vowed to never enlighten him on the matter.

But to not remember ever having been hugged…that was heartbreaking, too.

She'd simply have to keep her heart secure while Sawyer found himself again. The last thing she needed was to fall for Sawyer just in time for him to remember all the reasons they'd never worked.

Later that morning, Sawyer followed Lloyd's pickup, keeping a safe distance back as they rumbled through the back roads. Lloyd knew how to get to the little country church, and Sawyer didn't. If he lost Lloyd, Olivia could probably direct him there, but it was the man in him that wanted to do this without her help.

These turns were confusing, but he watched carefully all the same, hoping to have a sense of the next turn before Lloyd's blinker started up. So far, nada.

He'd asked Lloyd about his church attendance before they left, and Lloyd had scuffed his boot in the dirt a bit and shrugged sheepishly.

"It's a chance at a fresh start, Sawyer. Church never hurt."

And maybe Lloyd had a point there.

In the back seat, the girls were babbling to each other, and Olivia sat next to him wearing her "one and only dress" that she'd brought along—a calf-length cream-colored dress that made her cheeks look a little pinker and her eyes that much warmer by contrast. She smelled good—like lilacs. She'd wrapped a floral patterned shawl around her, and he noticed her slim shoulders... He was glad that she looked decidedly different from that memory in the snowy street. He needed that—for her to be stronger now, brighter, further away from that heartbreaking day.

"Is any of this familiar?" Olivia asked.

"Nope."

He couldn't banish the guilt that he hadn't remembered Mia yet, either. He'd been her husband—it felt like a betrayal of sorts to have no memories of her. But at least a couple of things had started to resurface, and maybe his memories with Mia would come next.

Ahead, Lloyd signaled another turn and slowed. Sawyer followed suit and clicked on his blinker. As they eased around the corner, he could see a little white church ahead with a steeple.

He had that memory of the little wood-paneled room where Mrs. Willoughby had taught him Sunday school, but this church wasn't familiar at all. It was frustrating—so many memories just on the edge of where he could reach them.

He pulled into the parking lot, and there was something about that view as his truck eased over the crest of a bump—the church, the open doors, the sunlight splashing across the steps. It sparked something. It started with a feeling of familiarity, and then he got a flash of hands reaching out to shake his. He was wearing a black suit—he remembered that. But he hadn't seen a black suit in his closet earlier today when he was trying to find something to wear to church.

"Something happened here," he said, his heart speeding up.

Olivia didn't answer, but when he glanced toward her, she was looking at him with a strained expression on her face.

He remembered sunlight, and warmth. He remembered people reaching out to touch his arm—not his arm, the babies he held in his arms. People had been gently touching the babies, tears in their eyes. There was a glossy wooden coffin. "It was her funeral."

He remembered something of his wife... finally! And the realization was both a relief and a punch to the gut. He couldn't remember what she looked like, but he remembered the closed lid of the coffin, some fingerprints on the surface, a bouquet of flowers that someone had put on top. Other people must have been holding the babies for a while, because he remembered putting his hand out, his palm flat against the wood as grief tore through him.

Sawyer pulled to a stop next to his uncle's vehicle, and he let out a slow, shaky breath. Tears welled up inside of him, but he wouldn't let them through.

"Sawyer?" Olivia's hand touched his arm, and he turned off the engine, then let his hands drop.

"It's okay," he said. He didn't want to delve into that memory here. It was private, and he didn't want to let the lid off of those tears. But he had the memory—and he was holding on to it with everything he had.

"You remember Mia?" she whispered.

"I remember her funeral," he said huskily. "It's something."

His emotions clashed inside of him, and he looked over to see that Lloyd stood outside the church entrance, waiting for them. There were expectations here. Sawyer pushed open his door.

"You okay?" Lloyd asked, frowning and stepping closer. Maybe Sawyer wasn't so good at hiding his feelings, because Lloyd looked downright scared.

"Yeah, yeah..." Sawyer looked around, trying to center himself. He glanced back at the truck—the girls still in their car seats.

"She's buried in the churchyard," Olivia said quietly, and Sawyer looked past the church toward the graveyard beside it. "I could show you where—"

"No." It came out more gruffly than he'd intended. But he didn't want any company for this, especially not from someone he'd remembered before Mia.

"Why don't Olivia and I take the girls into church," Lloyd said. "And you can go...pay your respects."

It was like his uncle had read his mind, and Sawyer looked back into the truck window one last time to see Bella trying to reach her little shoe, and Lizzie chewing on a seat belt strap.

"It's fine," Olivia said quickly. "Come into

the church whenever you're ready. We'll sit in the back."

"Okay."

Sawyer met her gaze once more, and he could see sadness swimming there. She shrugged faintly. He nodded, acknowledging the gift of some time alone that she was giving him. Then he started off across the gravel parking lot toward the graveyard. He didn't remember it, but if Mia was buried there, he'd find her. And maybe with the grave, he'd get some peace.

He could hear the babble of his daughters behind him, the gentle tones of Olivia's voice. From inside the church, he could hear the sound of a piano filtering outside, and the tune sounded hauntingly familiar, but again, he couldn't quite place it.

The graveyard was fenced off with a low stone wall, and he walked around it to a narrow gate bearing a plaque etched with a verse:

Blessed are they that mourn: for they shall be comforted.

An ancient tree from outside the grave-yard stretched long branches out over the wall and provided a bit of shade. Most of the headstones this close to the fence were old, moss growing up the sides and the engravings tough to make out. Further back, the headstones got newer, and he walked in that direction. He scanned the names—Robert Eugene, Viola Travis, Candy Newhart... Did he know any of these people in his past? Had any of these people touched his life in some way? He strolled past the headstones, reading names and dates, pausing at a few that had his last name. Were they family? Probably. But he didn't remember any of them.

"Lord, let me remember," he whispered.

He'd read in Genesis that morning where God said that it wasn't good for man to be alone, and that void in his head where a life-time of memories were supposed to reside made him ache with loneliness. Except, he wasn't entirely alone. He had God. He had Lloyd, his little girls, and now Olivia—this mix of people by his side who kept telling him who he used to be. They'd loved him… or cared about him at least.

Walter West. That name tugged at something inside of him, something that smelled like Old Spice and hay. He looked at the dates. Could this be his father?

A flicker of a face teased in his mind—a man with a bushy beard and twinkling eyes. He was peeling an apple with a pocketknife, the peel winding down in a continuous coil.

Dad. He was certain of it now. This was his father's grave, and with it came some fragmented memories. A hand on his shoulder, a chipped coffee mug, a deep voice that was slow and quiet.

We'd best head back if we're gonna beat that weather.

Why would those words stick? Maybe his father had said them often. Sawyer rubbed a hand through his hair. But still, some memories were coming back. His memory wasn't in one piece, and it wasn't enough by far, but it was better than this strange emptiness he'd been carrying around.

Sawyer kept walking, and he scanned more names—Taylor, Grouse, McDonald... none of them ringing any more bells for him.

Then he spotted a small gravestone—a flat one. It looked newer than the others. He stepped closer and looked down at the inscription: "Mia West. Beloved wife, young mother, adored daughter. Rest in peace."

This was hers—Mia's resting place—and his heart sped up. Sawyer crouched down next to the stone and brushed a dried twig off of the smooth surface. His fingers lingered over the engraved name. He'd found her. He looked around himself, at the other gravestones, at the dappled shade left by that overhanging branch... There was a bench not too far off—a stone bench with an inscription to someone else.

"I'm sorry, Mia," he said quietly. "I'm trying so hard to remember you."

But maybe this was the right place to try.

He glanced toward the bench, then sighed and went over to sit down. He could see Mia's headstone from there, and he leaned back. The sun was warm, and without a breeze, it almost felt like summer. He was waiting to remember something like he had when he saw his father's stone—some fragment of memory, some glimpse of her face. But when he thought about her, all he could see were those wedding pictures from the album—the dark-haired woman with the pretty smile. The one who felt like a stranger. But he could remember the wave of grief he'd felt at her funeral. He could remember his own sense of loss.

How selfish did that make him, to only remember her for how her loss had affected him?

God didn't seem to be answering his prayer for a flood of memories. Instead, Sawyer sat in the quiet, his heart heavy and the sunlight warm against his legs. The minutes slipped by, and he realized that the music had stopped inside the church, and he could hear the rumbling drone of a voice—the preacher, maybe?

"Let me remember her, Lord," he prayed, but there was no immediate answer.

Footsteps on the cement pathway made him look up, and he saw Olivia. She walked slowly in his direction, then paused when she got closer, giving him a hesitant smile.

"Where are the girls?" he asked.

"There are two teenage girls there who have been feeding them Goldfish crackers. They're all blissfully happy, teenagers and toddlers alike."

"Right." There would be people who knew his daughters better than he did right now.

"I see you found her," Olivia said.

"Yeah... I did." He scooted over on the bench a few inches, and Olivia came over and sat down next to him.

"How much do you remember?" she asked.

"Not a lot. I remember the funeral, mostly. Just some snapshots of memory. I'm trying to drag up more, and I'm not having a lot of success."

"Do you remember me being at the funeral?" she asked.

"No, I don't remember that. You were there?"

"Of course I was there. She was my best friend."

Sawyer looked over at Olivia and saw the sadness in her eyes. It was a tempered grief, though. Time had started healing things for her. Had it done the same for him?

"There is one thing I really regret, though," Olivia went on.

"What's that?"

"I didn't come to her grave," she said, her voice quiet.

"Why not?"

"A lot of people came to her funeral— some of them had been horrible to me. I just wanted to get away, I guess. I shouldn't have left without seeing it, though. I regretted that."

Sawyer reached over and took Olivia's hand in his. Her fingers were soft, and she gave his hand a squeeze. He smiled, looking down at her small, pale hand in his broad, work-hardened palm.

She was a comfort, and he liked having her here with him, this close.

"I guess we're starting over, you and I," Sawyer said.

"No, we aren't," Olivia said, her voice trembling slightly. She pulled her hand back out of his grip, and he closed his fingers over his empty palm. Had he made a mistake there?

"I shouldn't have done that—" he started.

"Sawyer, it hasn't changed," she said with a shake of her head. "I can't stay in Beaut."

He was silent. What would he do when she left again? But he knew he had no right to ask her to stay. She was supposed to be helping him remember his life with Mia. He had no business getting attached to her like this.

"You said there were rumors," he said. "What kind?"

She looked over at him, her eyes filled with pain. "That I'd slept around. I hadn't, but no one would believe me. I was the target for every bully and gossip in my senior year of high school. I tried to ignore it, but there were a few boys who were making up these disgusting stories…" She sighed. "And it didn't change, either, after I graduated. People believe what they want to believe."

"It's been a while, though, hasn't it?" he asked. "People forget. Or lose interest. Or grow up a bit."

"This town has a long memory." She sighed. "When I came back to help my mom, I saw one of the girls who'd been awful to me—a grown woman at that point—and she said something snide about women 'like me.' It was couched in some Christianly inquiry into how I was doing, and hoping I'd found a husband after all of that. I had to hold myself back from slapping her. You've never seen a smugger woman in your life when she looked down at my left hand and saw there was no ring. There are people in life who want nothing more than to watch you fail—and in my life, they all live right here. My mother was dying, and it still didn't stop."

"Sounds like plain old bullying," he said.

She shrugged. He didn't remember any of this, obviously, but it made his blood simmer to think about that kind of cruelty. Olivia hadn't deserved that—he was certain. And a so-called Christian woman had rubbed those malicious rumors in her face? It was disgusting.

"I'm sorry," he said at last. "I wish I could do something—"

"You can't. And you have nothing to be sorry for," Olivia said. "You were a break from all of that. But the rest of Beaut owes me more than an apology."

"Is that why you came out here instead of staying in church?" Sawyer asked.

"No." She shot him a rueful smile. "I came out because I saw my brother in there. And I panicked."

Chapter Five

Olivia hunched her shoulders against a chilly breeze. She didn't like going over those painful memories, but coming back to Beaut seemed to make avoiding them impossible. Besides, those rumors had made things tough on her brother, too. He'd been teased about his sister. When she left for college, she'd thought that he would have been glad to see her go—leave him in peace—but instead, he seemed to feel like she'd abandoned him with all of it. And maybe she had. Maybe she deserved his resentment.

She had seen her brother in the service, sitting on the far side of the sanctuary. He was a few pews ahead, and at first she hadn't rec-ognized him. She certainly hadn't expected to see him in a church, of all places. But then he'd leaned over to whisper something to the woman sitting next to him, and Olivia had seen his profile.

Her escape outside had been cowardly on her part. If he was in church, maybe things were changing inside of him. Maybe he'd fi-nally found God! But she hadn't been ready to face Brian…or to have him simply turn away from her. Not in front of all those peo-ple.

The church doors opened, and a couple of people came outside. Then a few more. The service was over. She looked over at Sawyer.

"I wish you remembered Brian. Then you could tell me what you thought about my sit-uation with him. You never had any trouble pointing out where I was wrong."

"So, I was a bit of a jerk?" he asked hesi-tantly.

"No, you were honest. And generally, right,"

she replied. "I could count on you to tell me the truth, even if it was uncomfortable."

There had been a time when she and Mia had had a falling out. Mia had been upset with Olivia for missing a Christmas party at her parents' place—back when the Whites still lived in Beaut. Olivia hadn't thought it was a big deal, but it was Sawyer who'd pointed out that Mia had needed the emotional support at that party. Her parents could be hard on her. Sawyer had seen the root of the problem, and Olivia hadn't.

"Maybe it's better I don't remember him," Sawyer said. "I'm not the one you need to talk to."

"That is frustratingly wise of you," she said, then sighed.

"Yeah, it is, isn't it?" He shot her a teasing grin.

That was the old Sawyer there—the one from their single days. And she realized with a melancholy rush that she missed him, even now, because this wouldn't last, either. Whatever this time was without Sawyer's memory, this strange little oasis in the middle of their complicated history, would end, too.

The two teenage girls came out the church doors with Bella and Lizzie, followed by Lloyd. Olivia and Sawyer stood up.

"Back at it, then," Sawyer said quietly.

"You're doing well, Sawyer," she said. "You're a good dad, you know."

"I'm trying real hard," he replied.

The toddlers and their minders headed toward them, and Olivia looked up just as her brother came outside. Her brother was a shorter man, thin and wiry. He was wearing jeans and a T-shirt, more dressed down than the others coming outside. But he was good-looking in a way that the girls had always appreciated. Maybe it was his confidence. The young woman holding his hand was about an inch taller than he was in her heels, and she was slim, too, with long blond hair that fell loose down her back. Brian's gaze casually swept over them, then he froze, noticing her for the first time. Olivia swallowed and waved.

"Go on," Sawyer said. "Lloyd and I can handle the girls."

Olivia shot him a grateful look, and headed out of the graveyard toward her brother.

Brian murmured something to his girlfriend, but he didn't make any move in Olivia's direction. Brian and the young woman just waited until Olivia reached them.

"Hi," Olivia said.

"Hey." Brian was curt. "Didn't know I'd see you here."

"Well—here I am." She forced a smile in the woman's direction and put out her hand. "I'm Olivia, Brian's sister."

"Hi, I'm Shari." She smiled and they shook hands. "Nice to meet you."

She seemed nice enough, and Olivia turned back to her brother. "Fancy seeing you here."

"Yeah, yeah." Brian cast her an annoyed look. "Shari's grandmother asked us to go— a real guilt trip about how she doesn't have much longer in this life and she wanted to have at least one church service with Shari there."

Olivia couldn't help but smile at Shari for

that one. "She must be good at the guilt trips, your grandmother."

"A pro." Shari chuckled. "So we came. Duty done."

"So, you aren't a Christian—" Olivia began.

"My sister is," Brian explained to Shari. "And no, Shari and I aren't into church. This was a favor to her grandmother. End of story. No third degree."

"Oh." Olivia nodded a couple of times. "I left a few messages."

"I got them," he replied.

"Can we talk?" Olivia sighed. "Look, I know you're angry, but we can work through this."

"You don't even know what you did, do you?" he retorted, and Olivia felt heat rise in her cheeks. This was embarrassing.

Shari cast a mildly embarrassed look between Olivia and Brian, and then gave Brian's arm a squeeze.

"I'm going to just let you two talk," Shari said, and she moved away from them. Brian's gaze followed her as she moved on down the sidewalk. This girl wasn't just some girl-friend—she was special to Brian. She could tell by the way he looked at her.

"Shari seems nice," Olivia said.

"She is nice," Brian said, his gaze snapping toward her again. "Now, what do you want?"

"I want a conversation with you!" she said. "Brian, how long are you going to punish me for having gotten an education?"

Brian shook his head. "It's not your degree that makes me so mad. It's your whole attitude. This place was never good enough for you, and Mom just wanted to make you happy. She worked herself to the bone to scrape up money to keep you in school. Do you know how much she struggled to put you through?"

"I didn't know you wouldn't get your shot, Brian," she said with a shake of her head. "And you understand why I had to leave—"

"Yeah, because you misbehaved," he shot back, and Olivia had to shut her eyes to keep her temper under control.

"I didn't do what they said I did," she said,

her teeth clenched. "How many times do I have to tell you that?"

"Yeah, well, you were out at a bush party," her brother shot back. "And *something* happened..."

"I fought off a guy with a big mouth and embarrassed him! That's what happened!" she hissed.

A couple of people looked over their shoulders toward them. How much of their conversation was audible?

"So you walked away, spent every last penny from Mom, and left me here with all those rumors you didn't stick around and fight." Brian dug the toe of his shoe into the grass. "You know how that looked?"

"You think if I'd stayed in Beaut, it would have made them believe me?" she retorted. "Brian, quit being so naive!"

"I'm the naive one now?" He rolled his eyes. "So, if you don't think you did wrong by me, what about Mom?"

"I had to start my life, Brian," she said, her voice trembling.

"Yeah, well, great." Brian eyed her angrily.

"If I hadn't had my nursing degree—which I could only get in the city, by the way—I wouldn't have been able to take care of our mom toward the end," she added. "But these are old arguments. I left town, yes. I ran away from it all. But I had no idea our time with Mom was going to be so short. I didn't know you wouldn't get your turn at starting your life! What do you want from me?"

"I don't know," Brian replied. "You got the education. You got all the money. What do I want? Nothing! There isn't anything left for me! I've got this crippling debt hanging over me, and I can't get a loan without ridiculous interest rates. And they'd never give me enough to start my business. I had plans for my life, too, you know."

"I'm in debt, too!" she countered.

"But you've got your career. Do you know what Mom told me when I asked if she'd help me with some seed money for my business? She said she couldn't afford an extra penny, but when you were done, she'd focus on me. Well, that never happened, did it? She worked herself to death for you—"

"You can't blame cancer on me!" she snapped.

"Whatever. I'm not. I'm saying you got it all. Every last penny. Every last ounce of her strength. Congratulations."

They could bicker the same points for hours, but people were starting to look now, and Olivia caught her brother's arm and tugged him farther from the milling after-church crowd.

"I might have a solution to our money problem, at least," she said.

"How?" Brian frowned, and he pulled his arm free of her.

"I might have a way to get us out of debt a whole lot faster," she said. "And then we could get a small business loan for you—or I could work a bunch of overtime and put some money aside…"

"So you have a couple hundred thousand in your back pocket?" he asked skeptically.

"No. But Mia's parents have some clout with the hospital board, and they've asked me to help them reconcile with Sawyer. If I can make that happen, they'll talk to the right people and get our debt lowered considerably."

Brian stared at her, the information slowly sinking in. "By how much?"

"As much as possible. I don't know how much, exactly, but Mia's dad seemed pretty confident that he could make our lives a whole lot easier. That's why I'm back. But Sawyer had an accident that affected his memory, and he's really slowly getting it back. I have to wait until he can remember them before they can reconcile."

"He has amnesia?"

"Short term. Yeah. He's going to be okay, and his memory is coming back slowly, but he can't reconcile with people he doesn't remember yet."

"And the Whites are willing to help..." He still seemed stuck on that part.

"Brian, I'm doing my best here," Olivia said earnestly. "And if we could get that debt lowered, I'll put every extra penny into paying it off so you could be freed up to do whatever you want to do."

And he could stop resenting her for using up the last of the family resources. Brian's gaze moved toward Shari again, and Olivia watched him for a moment.

"She's special to you, isn't she?" she asked.

"Yeah." He heaved a sigh. "And she deserves more than what I can offer."

"She looks like she's just fine with what you can offer," Olivia said with a low laugh. "Any woman who wouldn't take you because you're not rich enough isn't worth having."

"That's not it," Brian said, shooting her an irritated look. "If it were only the two of us, it wouldn't be a big deal, but—" His face colored slightly, and he licked his lips. "It's not going to be just the two of us for much longer."

"Wait—" Olivia's gaze flickered toward the other woman. "Is Shari pregnant?"

"Yeah. And of all people, you don't get to lecture me about that."

"I'm not lecturing," she said, but her heart

clenched just a little. He still believed the rumors, didn't he?

"This wasn't exactly the plan." Brian sighed. "It just…happened. And I hear Mom's voice in the back of my head constantly, so I don't need any additional yelling."

"Congratulations," Olivia said quietly. "I think Shari seems great, and you should probably put a ring on that pronto."

"With what money?" he retorted.

"A cheap ring," she said with a weak shrug. "Who cares? You love each other. You're going to be parents. So get married already! *That* is what Mom would have wanted."

"I only just met her parents," Brian said. "And they're nice and all, but her dad is pushing me to do more with myself."

Pushy in-laws seemed to be a bit of a theme lately, and Olivia felt her stomach tighten. Who were these people to tell Brian he wasn't doing enough?

"Don't let them push you around," Olivia whispered.

"They're her parents. They have certain expectations for her."

Yeah, so had Mia's parents. They'd wanted her to marry a politician or a doctor. Instead, she'd fallen in love with a ranch hand. They'd been furious. But their ultimatums had backfired, because she married Sawyer anyway, and they were the ones who'd missed out on a relationship with her.

"What does Shari want?" Olivia countered. "That's what matters here."

"She wants a wedding," Brian said. "The kind of wedding she's dreamed of since she was a little girl. She wants all her friends and family there, and she wants this designer gown, and..."

"Traditionally, the bride's family pays," she said.

"That's old-fashioned. I don't want to be the guy who's forever beholden to her parents. It's a bad start."

"Okay," Olivia said. "But there's a difference between what we dream of and what's realistic. I'm sure she knows that."

"She doesn't know how much you and I owe that hospital, so..."

He hadn't told her... Her stomach sank.

"Then tell her," Olivia said, lowering her voice. "Even if the Whites help us reduce it, you have to tell her about it. Don't start out with secrets. Besides, there's a baby on the way. You don't have the time to rethink whether she's the one."

"Yeah, well, I have a feeling she'll be a bit disappointed when she finds out that the big wedding isn't a possibility," he replied, but his gaze softened. "Not really the way I want her to feel. Do you actually think Mia's parents will help us out?"

She could feel the hope in the air, softening Brian's stony attitude. Hope made all the difference, especially if her brother was about to be a father. Her little brother...

"They've promised they would," Olivia replied. "Brian, I've been praying and praying about that debt. I really think this is an answer to that prayer. They want to know their granddaughters, and they're willing to help us if I can help them. I know you got the short end of the stick, but if we could get rid of this debt, then I'll help you get that business loan." She smiled hopefully.

"Yeah?" Brian asked hesitantly.

"Yeah. That's a promise." Olivia looked over to see Shari standing a few yards off, watching them. "She's waiting for you."

Brian's gaze followed hers toward his girlfriend. "I want to give my kid more than we had. If Dad hadn't left—"

"You aren't leaving your child," Olivia said firmly. "Your baby will already have more than we did, because he or she will have both parents. This baby is good news, Brian. Really good news. I'm happy for you."

"Okay, well…when do you take care of your side of things?" Brian asked. "When do you talk to Sawyer about it?"

"When he remembers enough," she replied. "I can't rush that. It wouldn't be right to pressure him when he's at his most vulnerable. As soon as he remembers the situation, I can tell him that they want to make up. But until then…"

"Yeah, I get it," Brian agreed. "Keep me posted."

"You'd better pick up my calls then," she retorted.

Brian didn't answer that, but he did give her a small smile. Then he headed toward Shari and caught her hand in his. It was a start—and if the Whites could make good on their promise, Brian would get his chance to pursue his goals. She'd make sure of it. She wouldn't be the only one to get the life she'd dreamed of.

It didn't take Sawyer and Olivia too long to get the toddlers into their car seats. The little girls were in a good mood. Lloyd stood off to the side talking to a remarkably beautiful young woman next to his truck, and he didn't look like he was in much of a hurry to leave. The woman was tall, slim, with dark hair…and she leaned in when Lloyd spoke to her. Sawyer glanced over at Olivia sitting next to him. She looked sober, a little pale, too. Was she okay?

The toddlers were babbling to each other in their car seats, and Bella let out a shriek of annoyance. He looked back at them.

"What?" he asked. He wasn't sure what he was expecting—an answer? Not really—but Bella squirmed in her seat and wailed again. Olivia turned around to look, too.

"Oh—" Olivia stretched and picked up a fallen sippy cup and handed it to Bella, who popped it into her mouth and started to drink.

"Thanks." Sawyer shot her a smile, then looked toward Lloyd, who was still standing outside of his truck chatting. "Lloyd doesn't look like he's in any hurry. We could leave without him."

"Or we could see who he's flirting with. I don't know her—and she doesn't look local. She looks…city." Olivia chuckled.

"I think *she's* the one who's flirting," Sawyer countered. But a woman like that—she wouldn't be interested in an old rancher Lloyd's age, would she?

"So, how did it go with your brother?" Sawyer asked, glancing toward her.

"Good," Olivia said. "I think so, at least."

"You talked for a bit," he said.

"We did." She leaned back in the seat. "It's still pretty tense, but he's my brother. Nothing is going to change that, and I like to think that he might need a little more of me now."

"Why's that?" he asked.

She eyed him for a moment. "Can you keep a secret?"

"Could I before?" he asked jokingly.

"Like a vault," she replied with a chuckle.

"Then I probably can," he replied. "What's going on?"

"My brother's girlfriend is pregnant."

"Pregnant!" Sawyer raised his eyebrows. "Wow. So...is this good news?"

"Yes," she said with a decisive nod. "I mean, obviously, it wasn't the order he'd wanted to do things, but a baby is always good news. And Shari really seems nice. He's smitten."

"Great. So, what's next for him, then?"

"A wedding, I hope," she replied. "At least that's what I'm encouraging him to do. But it's a bit complicated. He doesn't have a lot of extra money, and she's got her heart set on a dream wedding. There isn't a lot of time to save up. Her parents might offer to cover it but he doesn't want to be the guy who sailed through on someone else's dime. It's a matter of pride."

"Yeah, I could see that," he replied. Even without his memory, he could understand wanting to avoid that. A man had to be able to look himself in the mirror, after all. Independence mattered—something that was chafing at him now that he was functioning without his memory.

"Did I let Mia's parents pay for my wedding?" he asked hesitantly.

"No, you and Mia had a really modest event. And her parents weren't at your wedding," Olivia said, and her gaze flickered toward him hesitantly. There was more to that—he could tell.

"Why?" he asked.

"Uh—" She sighed. "They hadn't exactly given their blessing."

"I wasn't good enough?" he asked, and Olivia's cheeks colored. So that was it. "What was wrong with me?"

"Back then, it was less about you personally and more about their hopes for her future. They were climbing and they wanted their daughter to marry up, so to speak."

"So it was a money thing?" he asked, the words tasting sour in his mouth.

"More or less," Olivia replied with a sigh. "But they've changed now. They aren't the same."

"It probably doesn't matter too much since I haven't seen them around. Where are they?"

"Billings...and DC. They travel between the two. He's a senator."

So, he'd married a senator's daughter... He wouldn't have guessed that. Sawyer sifted through these new details, looking for some memories to attach them to. There wasn't anything.

"Do I ever see them?" he asked.

"Not since the funeral, no." Her words were cautious.

"Olivia, just tell me what happened!" he said, exasperated. "I can't play Twenty Questions with you. I don't know what to ask."

She looked over at him, then sighed. "You and Mia fell in love. Her parents wanted her to marry another up-and-coming politician who was sweet on Mia, but she'd chosen you. They refused to go to the wedding, and it was stony silence after that."

"But they were at the funeral."

"Yes," she confirmed. "They had only found out about your daughters when Mia passed away. They hadn't even known she was pregnant. They were really upset. They thought that if they'd at least known, they could have provided access to better doctors, and all that. They thought maybe she would have survived the birth… It wasn't fair of them to say that, but tensions were running high and everyone was very emotional. They'd lost their only child, remember. They were wrecks. You were furious—understandably. They left again, and you haven't spoken to them since."

Her words hit him in the gut—they thought Mia might have survived if they'd been able to help...

"Were they right?" he asked. "If they'd been able to provide better doctors..."

"No," Olivia said quickly. "She was at the hospital. She had quality doctors. It wasn't that. They know that, too. They just overreacted in the heat of the moment. But you didn't talk to me about it much."

"Because we were still distant with each other."

"And because I was...close with them." Color tinged her cheeks.

"So you chose them..."

"No, but they were my best friend's parents! I knew them. We were all grieving for her. And you didn't understand my relationship with them. So...you and I drifted apart for more than one reason."

So in essence, yes, when pushed, she'd

chosen them. He wasn't sure how he felt about this right now. He looked over at Olivia, and she gave him an agonized look.

"That's why, when you didn't recognize me, I thought maybe you were just punishing me still," she said. "There never should have been sides to begin with. You were all a family."

Sawyer didn't answer. Whatever had happened back then sounded painful. He hadn't thought to question where Mia's family had been in his life—at least not until now. So they'd rejected both him and Mia, because he hadn't been up to par. That stung, even now. What he did know about himself was that he'd worked hard. He was told he'd been honest and loyal. Hadn't any of that mattered?

"Does any of this sound familiar at all?" she asked.

"No," he admitted. "I don't remember it."

"Okay..."

She was waiting for something from him, and he rolled this new information over in his mind, wondering if it changed anything. He didn't have many memories of their past relationship to go on besides wanting to hug her in the street, but her compassion, her patience, her kindness, had all made a huge difference for him over the last couple of days. He felt like he knew her well enough to trust her intentions, at the very least.

"Look, I think I understand," he said after a moment. "It was complicated, and you were doing your best. I guess you were kind of stuck in the middle. But you're here now, and I really appreciate it. So…let's just leave it at that."

"Sure." She nodded. "And I want you to know that our friendship does mean a lot to me. I care."

Whatever had been between them before— that spark that had begun their friendship— was still there. And he could see why they'd gravitated toward each other to begin with. She meant something to him, too. Again.

"I *am* on your side," she added. "I always have been, even when it was complicated."

"I think I know that," he replied gruffly. He wasn't sure what else to say, how to encompass these softer feelings in words.

"Good." She smiled. "Just for the record, I guess."

He leaned back, stretching his arm out straight to rest the heel of his hand on top of the steering wheel. Lloyd seemed to have finished up his conversation because the woman smiled at him and headed off toward another vehicle. Lloyd looked in her direction for a moment, then glanced uncomfortably back at Sawyer in the truck.

Sawyer lifted two fingers in a salute, and Lloyd's face turned pink. Sawyer couldn't help but chuckle as Lloyd got into his own truck and started the engine.

Sawyer was glad that Olivia was here. Like following Lloyd in that pickup truck ahead of him along these back roads, Olivia was helping him navigate his way back home again. As much as he wanted to be able to do this on his own, he couldn't. He needed help, and he was glad help had shown up in the form of this old friend.

"So, you're going to be an aunt," he said with a small smile, starting the truck.

"I'm going to be an aunt." She smiled back, and it was more relaxed this time.

It seemed that God had provided for him before he even knew what to ask. Maybe in some small way, He'd provided for both of them. Because Sawyer wanted to help her. Even if that was just sitting there and listening when she needed to talk.

Chapter Six

Sawyer sat at the kitchen table the next morning, his Bible in front of him and his gaze locked on the side door. He was frustrated. He had no memory of how to do the work that used to occupy him, but his muscles seemed to remember having done something other than this easy-paced recovery. And he was itching to exert himself. In fact, he was eager to get out there and actually work. It would come back to him—other memories had been resurfacing. Why not his job?

This was what he had—his hard work. That was one thing he'd heard over and over again—and he could see the evidence on his calloused hands. He might not have been half-good enough for a lot of women, but at least he'd been a hard worker. There was a lot of stuff outside of a man's control, but his work ethic wasn't one of those. He could choose how hard he worked—and that could define a man.

So being stuck in the house with his little girls was grating on him—as awful as that sounded. He loved them already, and he could remember a few little details about them now, like the way their newborn hair had swirled. He couldn't remember anything else about those early days, but he remembered the tops of their heads. So this wasn't about not loving his girls, it was about something deeper—his own need to put his muscles into some good, hard work, and loosen himself up again.

Lloyd's footsteps sounded on the steps outside, and the door opened. The older man came inside, pulled off his hat and rubbed a hand over his forehead.

"Another twelve calves since last night," he announced. "And one had triplets."

"Yeah?"

"Rare—it doesn't happen too often. All three survived, too. The smaller two will have to be bottle-fed, but the bigger one is feeding fine."

Sawyer nodded, then rose to his feet. "Coffee?"

"Please." Lloyd pulled off his boots, then headed for the sink.

"Did you get my text?" Sawyer asked.

"Yeah. My answer is no."

Sawyer heaved a sigh. "It'll come back to me, Lloyd. I know it."

"You've had a head injury," his uncle retorted. "We've been over this! I mean…" His uncle faltered and looked at him over his shoulder. "Do you remember us discussing that?"

"Yes, I remember it," Sawyer said irritably. "I'm antsy. I need to do something."

His uncle washed his hands, silent through

the process, then grabbed a towel and slowly turned.

"You've got a real chance here to start over," Lloyd said slowly.

"A chance?" he said with a short laugh. "I have no other choice. That's what I'm trying to do—get back to where I was before."

"But you've got a chance to do things differently. We don't all get that."

Sawyer eyed his uncle uncertainly. "Like, how differently? From what I can figure, I worked hard and I did a good job. That's what you told me, isn't it?"

"Yep, that's true."

"So why would I want to change? Let me learn that again. I feel like a coiled spring. I'm going nuts here."

Lloyd regarded him for a moment, hesitating. Then he sighed. "We all have our faults. For me, I never took risks. I lived to regret it, you know. I look back on my life and I see times when I should have stepped up and done something. I should have put myself out there. I was always more afraid of rejection than I was of just not trying. I was more comfortable with cattle than people... than women."

"Was I...like that?" Sawyer asked.

"I'm talking about me. I'm saying, *I* have regrets," Lloyd replied. "I never got married. I knew I was kind of funny-looking, and I took a few well-aimed insults to heart. Eventually I just stopped asking girls out." He laughed uncomfortably. "You used to know about this. I don't know what I thought would happen, but here I am. I'm fifty and single. I don't have a wife, or kids of my own. I was honored to take you in after your dad passed, don't get me wrong. But I was too scared to make a life of my own. Too scared I'd put my heart out there and get turned down."

"But you said I had the chance to start over," Sawyer prodded. "What are my regrets that I don't remember?"

"I'm not judging, Sawyer," his uncle replied quietly. "But you're like me in a lot of ways. You buried yourself in work instead of really living your life. Every extra minute, you were out there trying to build this ranch into something bigger. Like you had something to prove to yourself. And you had a good woman here—she loved you and she understood your drive, but when you get to be my age, you don't look back on those years and regret not having worked harder. You regret the time you didn't spend with the ones you loved."

His hard work—had it gone overboard?

"I...neglected my wife?" Sawyer asked, frowning.

"She understood, but your daughters might not," Lloyd said, and he shrugged apologetically. "That's all I'm saying. Those little girls are going to grow up whether you're around to see it or not. And they'll have a few resentments of their own if they feel like you weren't there for them. Maybe this loss of memory can give you a chance to start fresh—take more breaks. Whatever was pushing you before, doesn't have to push you now."

"Olivia told me that my in-laws thought I

wasn't good enough for their family. Didn't even come to the wedding, apparently. And they cut Mia off for having married me." Sawyer paused, swallowed. "So maybe I did have something to prove."

"Who cares about the opinions of some hoity-toity politician types?" his uncle demanded. "Yes, it got under your skin, but people will have opinions about you. You'll have a few about them, too. But other people's ignorant biases don't have to define you. You need to recover, and you need time with your children. Maybe forgetting a few things is a blessing. Ever thought of that?"

"You said you were the same as me," Sawyer said irritably.

"I am," Lloyd replied. "I let other people's opinions hobble me for decades. And I'm not letting it stop me anymore. I might be late to the dance, but I'm here now."

"What does that mean?"

"It means, I want a wife," Lloyd replied. "I

might be a lot of things, but I'm still a man. And I want a woman by my side."

Was that what that long conversation with the woman at the church had been about— another chance at romance?

"Okay..." Sawyer eyed his uncle. There was sympathy in those steel-blue eyes. And wisdom.

"You can change, too," Lloyd said. "You've got a God-given opportunity here to start fresh. Don't squander it."

Sawyer looked away from his uncle, frustration rising inside of him.

"I appreciate the warning," Sawyer said after a moment. "But I need to do something—anything—useful."

Lloyd heaved a sigh, then looked out the kitchen window. "You see the vegetable garden?"

"Yeah." He'd seen it. He'd been staring moodily at it for the last few days.

"It needs a good weeding again," Lloyd said.

Weeding the garden... Not exactly what

he'd been thinking of. He'd hoped for something that would take his whole concentration and distract him from the way his mind was still grabbing at elusive memories. When he did retrieve a few, what would he discover? He wanted his past back, his history. But he hadn't stopped to consider that he'd also be getting his regrets back as well.

Sawyer was silent for a moment, then he rose to his feet, heading for the window. He looked out over the vegetable garden. He could recognize the first sprouts of carrots and lettuce. There were other rows he didn't know immediately.

"Okay," Sawyer said. "It's something."

Lloyd pulled a bowl from the fridge and put it into the microwave. He punched some buttons and it whirred to life.

Sawyer watched his uncle amble about the kitchen, his mind spinning. He'd assumed that his hard work had meant he was a good man, a worthy man. But he was beginning to see a different side to his past—a different version of the story where his hard work had gotten in the way of his relationships.

"Lloyd, what kind of father was I?" he asked.

Lloyd turned back, then shrugged. "You loved your kids."

"But?" Sawyer prodded.

"You were a good dad, just busy. Preoccupied."

"Was I like that in my marriage, too?"

Lloyd sighed. "I've never been married, myself, so I'm no expert, and I don't pretend to be..."

"But Mia and I lived here—"

"In the manager's house. You and the girls moved up here with me after she died."

"Okay, but she must have talked to you," Sawyer said. "Right?"

"She might have mentioned a thing or two," Lloyd replied.

"Well?" he asked. "What did she say?"

"Instead of facing the stuff you didn't like to think about, you got it out of your system with ranch work," Lloyd replied quietly. "I can't judge. I did the same thing. But I didn't have a woman at home waiting on me. At least you were working and not out drinking or carousing."

"She wasn't quite so happy as a guy might hope."

"She was lonely," Lloyd confirmed.

Lloyd turned back as the microwave dinged, and he pulled the bowl out and peeled off the plastic wrap. It was reheated oatmeal, by the smell of it. Lloyd went about doctoring it up with sugar and milk, then took a dribbling bite.

"So, I messed things up," Sawyer said.

Lloyd looked up. "We all have our hang-ups. You had yours. The past can't be changed, so there's no sense in dwelling on it. But right now, those little girls need their dad more than you need to prove yourself to the Whites."

"Fine." He could grudgingly see his uncle's point. Lloyd was only trying to help—he knew that—but there was something funda-mental about Sawyer that even erasing his memory didn't change. Because even knowing that dedicating too much time to work had messed things up with his family didn't change his rising frustration and his desire to be outside with dirt under his boots and get something done.

Anything.

Work might have been his solace before the accident, but his eagerness to get back to it wasn't only about proving himself to the in-laws he no longer remembered. Because even without that goading, his gaze kept moving to the window, beyond the fence and to the fields beyond.

He knew where he belonged—out there.

What did that say about him?

The toddlers woke up as soon as Olivia exited the bathroom, and the house appeared to be empty, so she lifted them out of bed, got them changed and dressed into matching jeans and little sweaters, and brought them out to the kitchen. She spotted Sawyer through the kitchen window, a hoe in hand as he bent over the garden bed. He paused, picked something out of the dirt, then tossed it aside onto the grass and continued his hoeing once more.

She watched him for a moment, then looked down at the girls, who were playing with that bucket of toys in the corner.

"Daddy is outside," Olivia said.

The girls glanced up at her, then turned back to their playing. She opened the side door and went out onto the step where she could see Sawyer bend down again, pick a rock out of the soil and toss it to the side. Then he set back to work. There was another clang as his hoe hit a rock.

"What are you doing?" Olivia called from the side door.

Sawyer looked up and wiped his forehead with the back of one hand. "Working."

"Do you need a hand?" she asked.

"Nope."

With a head injury like his, it wasn't wise for him to be exerting himself just yet. There was a lot of unseen healing that needed to happen, but she doubted he wanted to hear that—not when she could feel the irritability coming off of him in waves.

"Your daughters are awake," Olivia said, glancing back into the kitchen. The toddlers came toward the open door and poked their heads out.

"Daddy!" Bella called.

Sawyer scrubbed a hand across his face and looked over at them, his expression grim.

"Would you mind watching them for a bit?" he asked.

Did she mind spending time with two little cuties? Not at all. But these little girls didn't need her, they needed their dad. Besides, with her medical experience, she knew he shouldn't be exerting himself like that right now.

"You should be resting," she said.

"I need to get busy. I'm going stir-crazy," he replied.

Bella and Lizzie squeezed past her out the door, but Olivia caught them before their socked feet hit the dew-laden grass. She carried them back inside and dropped them both into their rubber boots. Then she released them so they could clomp back outside again. Their sweaters would be warm enough for now. The toddlers headed in their father's direction. She saw his expression soften at the sight of them, but the tension was still there.

"They want you, not me," she said. "Besides, this isn't good for you."

"Says who?" he snapped, then he sighed. "Look, I'm sorry, but I need this."

In the hospital, she was used to ornery patients, but in the emergency room, they were normally in too much pain to put up much of a fight. She was responsible for helping sew them back together, and she wasn't the one who kept them from overdoing it through the slow days or weeks of healing.

"You're recovering," she said curtly.

"My memory is coming back. I remember enough not to hit myself in the head with a hoe."

"You're recovering physically, too. Your

doctor would have told you to relax for a couple of weeks, right?"

He shot her an annoyed look. "You aren't my nurse."

"Nope, but I said I'd help. This is my way of doing that," she said. "What's going on?"

"Nothing is going on. I'm tired of just sitting around feeling lost and confused. I was hoping you'd watch the girls so I could vent some frustration here."

"What are you frustrated about?" she asked. "Maybe I can help."

"Everything!" He sighed. "Nothing. You and Lloyd seem pretty focused on keeping me from working. But getting back to it is what's going to make me feel better, okay? Can you keep an eye on them, or not?"

"And if I say no?"

Sawyer stopped, eyed her uncertainly. "Are you saying no?"

Olivia didn't want to turn this into a power struggle. She sighed. "I'll watch them. But if you end up back in the hospital because you overdid it, you'll only have yourself to blame."

"Yeah, but I won't remember that," he said irritably, and she could hear the dry humor in his voice.

"Har har," she muttered.

But she wasn't joking. Head injuries were nothing to play with, especially ones severe enough to cause amnesia. Olivia turned her back on him and headed toward the house, then sat down on the step so she could watch both the girls playing and their father.

Sawyer looked over his shoulder. "So you're just going to stare at me?"

"Might as well," she replied.

She knew she was irritating him, but right now she didn't care. He was risking his health by pushing it, and while she could sympathize with his frustration, she was frustrated, too.

Sawyer picked up the hoe again, and as he did, he winced, gritted his teeth and looked down at his palm.

"What?" she called.

"Nothing." He grimaced, looked at the wooden handle of hoe, then back at his hand.

"Liar," she said with a low laugh.

"It's a splinter." He raised his hand, but she couldn't make anything out from where she sat, so she pushed herself back to her feet and headed across the grass toward him. When she arrived at his side, she took his fingers in her hand to get a better look. A long, dark shard had shoved itself deep under the skin of his palm.

"That would hurt," she said, grimacing.

Sawyer tried to pinch the end with his fingernails, and Olivia slapped his hand away.

"Cut that out," she said. "You'll only break it off and it'll be that much harder to get the rest of it."

"I think I can—" Sawyer turned away from her a little bit to try and grab it again, and she swatted his arm.

"You'll make it worse," she warned. "That's more than a splinter. That's just about a stab wound."

He shot her an irritated look. "It's a splinter."

"Then go ahead." She crossed her arms over chest. "Let's see who's right."

She raised an eyebrow, and he met her gaze, then looked down at his palm. Blood had appeared at the site of the puncture. Olivia had dealt with similar small injuries at the hospital, and when the patient had mucked around, trying to pull the shard out themselves, it always made the retrieval process that much harder…and more painful.

"You said I was the bossy one," he muttered.

"I didn't say you were the *only* bossy one," she replied with a slow smile. "I'm a nurse. It comes with the territory. I'm also right most of the time. You hate that, for the record. But it doesn't change facts."

Sawyer smiled reluctantly. "I do hate this."

"Me being right, or just the whole situation?" she asked.

"Mostly you being right," he said, but his steely gaze had relaxed, and he glanced over to where the toddlers where playing by the fence.

"Come inside. You've got to have a first aid kit around somewhere."

Sawyer sighed. "Fine. We should grab the kids."

Sawyer headed after the girls. He scooped up one toddler with his good hand, and Olivia jogged over to gather up the other. Olivia had Bella in her arms, and the girl squealed, trying to wriggle free. Olivia managed to keep a hold of her, though, and when she stepped into the kitchen, she let Bella go. The girl beelined for the bucket of toys. Lizzie did the same when Sawyer put her down.

"So where's the first aid kit?" she asked.

"No idea." He looked around the kitchen, then shrugged.

Olivia pulled out her phone. Lloyd had given her his cell number earlier, and she typed in a text: Hi Lloyd. Just wondering where the first aid kit is. No emergency, so don't worry.

After a moment, there was a ping, and she read his reply.

"Top cupboard over the stove," she said. "Sawyer—sit down."

Olivia could reach the knob, and she tugged it open. The white plastic box was visible in the front of the cupboard, but when she stretched up, her fingers could only brush it when she went up onto her tiptoes. She'd need a stool or something. Sawyer sauntered up behind her, and when she dropped down to flat feet, she collided with his broad chest. He reached forward, over her head, and easily grabbed the box.

"I'm more useful than I look," he said, his voice a low rumble.

He was so close to her, those dark eyes boring into hers. Her breath caught, and for just a moment, he wasn't the old friend she could boss around. She didn't know this Sawyer quite as well as she'd imagined. Because this wasn't her buddy—this was a man who seemed to pin her to the spot with those dark eyes. This Sawyer didn't know their history, and yet even without it, they were drawn to each other. It hardly seemed fair. This wasn't supposed to get complicated...

Sawyer put the first aid kit into her hands, a half-smile tugging at his lips.

"Thank you," she breathed.

"You're welcome." He turned then, and headed to the table. He pulled out a chair with a scrape and sat down.

Their problem had never been a lack of chemistry. His gaze followed her as she came over to the table and opened the first aid kit.

"You need the rest, you know," she said pulling up a chair next to him.

"I don't want to rest," he replied.

"Sawyer, I get how frustrating this is," she said with a shake of her head. "I really do. But could you just not reinjure yourself on my watch? That's all I'm asking. After I'm gone, you're welcome to do any stupid thing you like. But if you get hurt while I'm supposed to be keeping you in one piece...people will talk, and I don't need more of that right now."

She shot him a teasing look, and he rolled his eyes.

"I'm not so vulnerable as you seem to think."

"This sliver begs to differ," she said, and pulled a pair of tweezers out of the first aid kit. "Now, hold your hand flat—hold your fingers down with your other hand...like that. Good."

She gave the sliver a little tug. It didn't budge. She tried again, and it moved ever so slightly. Sawyer winced.

"That hurts," he murmured.

"It would," she agreed, her voice low as she focused on grabbing the sliver again. "Keep an eye on the girls, would you? Accidents happen too easily..."

Sawyer's gaze moved toward his daughters, and as soon as his attention was off of his hand, she gave a pull and the rest of the sliver slid out of his flesh, a bead of blood filling up the wound.

"Ouch!" He pulled his hand back, but she

didn't let go of his fingers, tugging his hand back down to the tabletop.

"Stop that," she said, reaching for a cleansing pad. She used her teeth to tear the package open, and gently wiped the area. "Let me see if I got it all."

"So was that distraction there—telling me to watch the girls?" he asked.

"Bingo." She shot him a grin. She gave his hand one last stroke with the cleansing wipe, then reached for a bandage. "There. You're welcome."

Sawyer inspected his hand. "Thanks."

Bella came over to where her father sat and put a pudgy hand on his leg. "Up. Up!"

Sawyer picked her up and settled her on his lap. The toddler looked pleased with herself, and she leaned back against his shoulder.

"I need to get out there," Sawyer said quietly. "I'm going crazy. I need to do something…contribute."

Lizzie trotted over, a wooden block in one hand. She squatted down at Sawyer's feet and smacked his boot with the block. He looked down at her solemnly.

"There are more important things to do, Sawyer," Olivia said seriously. "Like remembering your daughters. You said you wanted to remember them, right?"

"I do," he agreed.

"Well, this is how you'll do that. And if, for some reason, you don't get those memories back, you're creating new ones."

Sawyer met her gaze and heaved a sigh. He looked down at Bella on his lap, then at Lizzie, who was heading back for the toy bucket. "You're very irritating when you're right."

"I know," she said. "I always did drive you nuts."

He smiled ruefully. "So this is just our dynamic, is it?"

"We always seem to fall back into it," she confirmed. Even when he couldn't remember their history, it seemed. This was how they'd always related to each other—relying on banter to cover over the deeper attraction they didn't want to talk about.

"I have a doctor's checkup this afternoon," he said. "Wondering if you might want to come along for that. I'm not real sure how to get there."

It was a good reason to bring her with him, but her stomach knotted up all the same. Did she want to go into town and face this community again? She'd seen another old acquaintance at the hotel—a cousin of a classmate who had pretended not to remember Olivia at all, even when she stopped to say hi. She could see in the woman's eyes that she knew exactly who she was, but the old games weren't over.

"Sure," she said, trying to sound casual. "A quick trip into town would be okay."

"We could bring the girls out for french fries or something afterwards," he said.

A little more than a quick trip, then. She sighed. "First, we need breakfast, though. Priorities."

Sawyer shot Olivia a smile, then looked

down at his daughter and ruffled her hair. "Deal. You hungry, Bella?"

That smile…it always had been able to crack her heart in two. But she wouldn't let herself fall for this man again. They hadn't been right for each other in the past, whether he could remember that or not. But she did remember what it felt like to watch him move forward with Mia. If she'd been able to make her peace with this town, Olivia would have been the one with Sawyer, not Mia. And watching Mia fall in love with him, watching Sawyer soften around another woman… It had been the hardest thing she'd ever had to do.

They'd been down this path before, and Olivia would just have to remember that for the both of them.

Chapter Seven

The drive into town felt a bit familiar, but Sawyer wouldn't have been able to navigate it himself. He hated that—the feeling of being dependent on another person to get him to a doctor's appointment. Maybe this was part of why he wanted to get out into the fields so badly—the independence. But if he couldn't find his way back home again, he could see the problem with that plan...

Independence would have to wait until his memory was back in full. Much as he hated it.

Sawyer drove and Olivia gave him directions. He'd been able to anticipate a couple of the turns, but once he got into town, he had no idea which way took him to the medical building on South Street. Olivia guided him to the parking lot in the back. She seemed tense again, and he looked over at her as he turned off the engine.

He was glad for the company because it made this appointment feel less intense. Truth be told, he was nervous about what the doctor would say. But after an examination, the doctor crossed her arms and nodded.

"You're coming along," she said. "You'll need more rest, but you'll heal. I'm glad to see how much of your memory has returned already. It's very promising. Just take it easy for a bit and give yourself the time."

"Is there anything I can do to hurry up the process?" Sawyer asked.

"Afraid not. Just some good old-fashioned rest. Can you manage it?"

"Yeah, I think so."

Everyone around him seemed pretty intent on making that happen, anyway.

"If you have any headaches, nausea, dizziness or increased confusion, come back," the doctor said. "Is there someone I can repeat that to who's with you today?"

Even the doctor was expecting him to have a babysitter with him.

"My friend, Olivia, is here," he replied. "She's an ER nurse, so..."

"Olivia Martin?"

"Yeah, that's her." Sawyer was mildly surprised, but maybe he shouldn't be.

"That's excellent. I'll walk you out and fill her in. But I'm pleased with your progress."

Olivia sat in the waiting room, holding a pile of blocks in her lap. For the moment, both Bella and Lizzie seemed focused on the blocks. After a brief hello, the doctor repeated her instructions, and they were allowed to leave.

"So you're doing well, then," Olivia said as she picked up Lizzie. Sawyer scooped Bella into his arms, and she settled against his chest, her animal-cracker-scented breath tickling his cheek. They paused to make sure they weren't forgetting anything, then headed for the door.

"Yeah, I'm doing fine," he said as they stepped outside, away from anyone who might overhear them. He felt more relieved about the doctor's diagnosis than he cared to admit right now. "Or I will be. I guess you were right about taking it easy."

"Amazing." She laughed and shot him a rueful look. "So you'll actually relax?"

"I don't know if I can promise that much," he retorted.

"Fine. I won't rub it in."

"Thanks." He adjusted his daughter in his arms as they stepped out into the cool afternoon air. "So why don't I buy you lunch? I feel like I owe you that much."

She nodded. "Sure. Thank you."

He scanned the street, looking at the shops: a dry cleaner, a card store, a jewelry store with a sale sign in the window… He was looking for some details to spark a memory—something to ground him. A diner up ahead felt familiar.

"What about that place? I feel like I know it."

"Yeah?" She was silent for a beat. "That's where I used to work as a waitress. Where we met."

So maybe that was a good place to start. Maybe he'd get back a few more memories while he was at it.

"Yeah, that sounds good. Lead the way," he said.

It felt oddly right to be walking down the street with Olivia at his side—like he'd done this before. She was comforting...but more than that, she just seemed to fit with him. His daughters had gotten attached to her, too, over the last few days. And while he didn't know if that was normal for them or not, it was a relief that his girls seemed happy.

What would it be like when she left again? She wasn't here to stay—she wasn't one of the regular parts of his life he could get accustomed to again, and he found himself wishing that she were.

As they approached the diner, Sawyer took in the wide front window, the faded, fluttering fabric of the awning, the sandwich board out front advertising the daily specials in chalk. It did seem familiar, and he felt a tremor of relief. It was coming back…a little at a time, but still.

He pulled open the door and a bell tinkled over their heads. Sawyer let Olivia go inside first. Lizzie had a handful of Olivia's curls in one pudgy fist, and Bella drummed on Sawyer's shoulder. Maybe the girls would like some fries or something. The diner was bright, everything seeming to be decorated in red vinyl. He looked around, the scent of fried food hitting his brain right in the pleasure center. He could see why he would have come here a lot. The stools by the counter seemed to ring a bell—the one at the end specifically. He used to sit there. He remembered a white mug of coffee, a burger and fries on an oblong plate…

"Hey, there."

A man about their age came out from the back, and gave them a cordial nod. He wore a white apron over jeans and a black T-shirt. The sleeves were rolled up to expose his muscled forearms. His face was scruffy, and he had the look of a guy who hadn't gotten enough sleep the night before. A toothpick quivered out the corner of his mouth when he talked.

"What can I get you?" he asked, then he squinted. "Wait… Olivia Martin?"

He looked from her to Sawyer. A flicker of recognition passed through the man's eyes, and he nodded toward Sawyer in a silent greeting.

Olivia stiffened, and Sawyer glanced down at her. Her smile had dropped and she gave the man a curt nod. Who was this guy…and should Sawyer know him? He didn't like the way Olivia had recoiled.

"Eddie Dane," Olivia said. It wasn't an exclamation. More like a grim announcement.

Bella put a hand on the side of his face, and

he patted his daughter's back absently. He felt a surge of protectiveness. It wasn't just Olivia here, but his daughters, too. Something felt off, and his hackles had gone up.

"Haven't seen you in a while," Eddie said with a slow smile. "These your kids?"

"No, they're mine," Sawyer said, forcing the other man to look at him. Sawyer met his gaze with the steely drill of his own—his own message of exactly how he felt about him.

"Hey, Sawyer," Eddie said. "Long time, man."

"Yeah." So apparently, he did know this guy. He didn't look worth remembering.

"Wow…" Eddie said, shaking his head. "I mean, I haven't seen you since high school. Senior year was pretty wild, huh, Olivia?"

"Not especially," she said dryly.

"Come on…" Eddie shot her a meaningful look. "I seem to remember you really came into your own that year."

"It's been a long time," she said pointedly. "I think we've all grown up since then, haven't we?"

"Oh, I don't know," Eddie said with a laugh. "I hope not too much. Where's the fun in that?"

The words themselves were innocent enough, but Sawyer sensed a meaning beneath the surface that irritated him. There was a familiarity on Eddie's side that felt like overstepping.

"I'm no fun," she retorted. "At all."

"I could change that..." Eddie leaned forward and gave her a slow smile. "You free tonight?"

"No," she said shortly, then she turned to Sawyer. "We should go."

A woman about their age came into the diner wearing a waitress uniform. She smiled in their direction, then came behind the counter and stashed her purse.

"Hi... Olivia?" She paused and a genuine smile broke over her face.

"Janice." Olivia forced a smile. "Hi. It's been a long time."

"Sure has. You look good."

"Thanks." Olivia relaxed a little.

"So, are you here to pay your brother's tab?" Eddie cut in.

"What?" Olivia turned back toward him. "What do you mean?"

"Brian's been running up a tab here for a year," Eddie replied with a shrug. "The owner says the next time he comes in, I'm supposed to throw him out."

"Norm said that?" she asked.

"Yeah. He only started that tab because Brian said you owed him money and that's why he was short. And Norm always was kinda sweet on you…"

"He was not sweet on me," she snapped.

"Whatever you say." That slow smile was back. "Norm doesn't do tabs, but he did one for your brother. You do that math. Anyway, Norm is done with him, so I figured maybe you came to pay up. Unless you missed me, or something."

Olivia blushed pink. She adjusted Lizzie in her arms.

"You want to cut that out?" Sawyer said, his tone menacing.

Eddie flatly ignored him.

"How much does Brian owe?" Olivia asked.

"I've got it here," Eddie said. "Hold on…"

He rummaged under the till and came out with a little book. "Two hundred and eighty-five."

He turned the book around in case Olivia didn't believe him, and Sawyer glanced at the tally of numbers over her shoulder. Sawyer pulled out his wallet and looked inside. He had about three hundred dollars in his wallet in fifties, and he realized he didn't know why he had that kind of money on him. Whatever—Olivia needed him right now, and he could sort out the rest later, he was sure.

Olivia opened her purse, but closed it without looking inside. "I don't have the cash on me right now. I could use a credit card."

"Norm doesn't take credit."

"Still?" She looked exasperated and heaved a sigh.

"I've got it," Sawyer said.

"Sawyer, you don't have to do that," Olivia said. "The bank is on the other side of town, but I'll be back in about twenty minutes and I'll pay it—"

"No, I've got it," Sawyer repeated. He pulled out the bills and put them on the counter.

Eddie counted the money and gave a nod. "I owe you some change." Then he glanced up at Olivia again. "So, you single? You look single to me."

Sawyer's ire rose at that question. It was the tone—oily and insinuating. It was obvious what Eddie thought of Olivia, and it took all of Sawyer's self-control to keep his mouth shut. But he was holding one of his daughters, and Olivia had his other girl in her arms. He felt hampered.

"Eddie, you are still a disgusting excuse for a man," she retorted.

"You used to be nicer!" the smaller man

snickered. "A whole lot nicer, to a whole lot of guys…"

"I never was *that* nice," Olivia said tersely. "Especially not to you."

"I know!" He laughed. "But I tried, didn't I? I'm definitely free tonight, by the way. You could get a piece of this." He spreads his hands, putting himself on display.

"That's rude, Eddie," Janice said curtly. "Are you still going on about that high school garbage? You're an idiot. Seriously!" She turned to Olivia. "For me, I'm sorry if I ever gave you a hard time, Olivia. I really am. Eddie should be, too."

"I'm joking," Eddie said. "Aren't I, Olivia?"

"Hey," Sawyer growled. "You keep that up, and you'll be dealing with me, personally."

Eddie's laughter evaporated and he shot Sawyer a nasty look. "Whatever."

While Eddie rang up the tab, Sawyer glanced down at Olivia beside him. Her face had gone from pink to stark white, and her eyes glittered with anger. Her grip on Lizzie had tightened, and she'd pressed her lips together into a line.

"Olivia…" he said softly. It felt good to finally be able to contribute something—even if that was a handful of cash. But there was something else going on here that he only partly understood. Something pointed and ugly, and it had hit its mark in Olivia.

"We're going to the bank, and I'm paying you back right now," she said, her voice low.

"Not necessary," he said.

"I'm paying you back," she repeated, this time with an edge to her tone, but when she glanced toward him, he saw tears mist her eyes.

When Eddie gave Sawyer his change, she blinked back the emotion.

"My brother won't be coming back here," she said curtly. "And I'll follow up with Norm, myself, and tell him that I've paid the bill. So don't try anything."

"I'm a witness," Janice said, coming up beside Eddie. "I saw you pay up in full."

Olivia and the waitress exchanged a look.

"Thanks," Olivia said. "I appreciate that."

"We women have to stick together, right? And he's a piece of work." She hooked a thumb toward Eddie.

"Hey, whatever..." Eddie put his hands up. "You staying to eat, or leaving?"

"Leaving," Olivia said curtly.

Olivia turned on her heel and headed for the door. Sawyer followed her, glancing over his shoulder at the man who stood behind the counter, muttering something under his breath. Sawyer might have known who the guy was before this stupid accident, but he was pretty confident that there were no conditions under which he'd actually like the guy. Olivia opened the door and held it until he grabbed it.

"Are you okay?" he asked as they hit the fresh air once more. The tinkle of the bell was muffled as the door swung shut behind them.

"No," she said, and her chin trembled. Then she clamped a hand over her mouth and squeezed her eyes shut as a tear escaped.

Oh, crud. He had a violent urge to go back into that diner and punch Eddie square in the jaw. But he was holding a toddler, and so was Olivia. So he did the only thing he could and planted his free hand on the small of her back and propelled her forward, away from the diner and back toward where the truck was parked.

"Let's go," he growled, tugging her close against his side. He didn't have a plan. He was moving on instinct right now, and everything inside of him was telling him to get her out of here.

He might not remember much, but he was still a man, and he wasn't letting her get insulted on his watch.

Sawyer's hand was warm against Olivia's back, and he guided her with the firm pressure of his fingertips. Olivia's heart was pounding, and she held Lizzie close as she did her best to match Sawyer's much longer strides. Noticing her struggles, he slowed, keeping in pace with her.

Eddie Dane, of all people… He'd just been some goofy loser in high school—he hadn't been a part of the original bullying that followed her all of senior year. But that just went to show how far those rumors had flown. This was why she'd had no other choice but to get out of town and start her life in the city—where there were enough people that one stupid rumor couldn't ruin a girl's life.

And yes, she'd pushed her mother to help her get away…she'd begged her mom to apply for those loans for her to go to Montana State so she could escape all the ugliness. For people like the Whites, that was no problem. For the Martins, it had taken everything they had. And it had left nothing for Brian. Anger mingled with guilt tangled up together inside of her.

"There—" Sawyer said, his voice close to her ear. "The park across the street."

Sawyer looked both ways, but Olivia's eyes were blurred with tears that she was still trying to blink back, and she followed him almost blindly as he led her across the road.

The park was small—just a slide, a couple
of swings and some benches surrounding
them. Sawyer took Lizzie from her arms and
Olivia sank onto the bench, watching as he
set the girls down next to the slide. He patted
it a couple of times. The toddlers looked at
him with that round-eyed curiosity of young
children, and then sat down on their bottoms
and reached for a couple of twigs.

When Sawyer slid onto the bench next to
her, he sat close enough that his leg pressed
against hers, welcome warmth on that chilly
day. She sucked in a stabilizing breath. She
was supposed to be here for him, not the
other way around. Besides, this was an old
problem that had already been solved by her
leaving town.

"So what was that?" Sawyer asked quietly.

Olivia looked over at him, but his gaze was
pinned to his daughters as they scratched in
the sand with their twigs.

"That's what I meant by this town having
a long memory," she replied.

"Do you want me to go back there and set

him straight?" he asked, and she eyed him for a moment to see how serious he was. He met her gaze evenly, and his jaw tightened.

"No," she said with a bitter laugh. "Eddie's not the real problem—and he's definitely not the only one. Connie Jenkins pretended she didn't know me when I first came into town."

"The waitress seemed to be nice, though," Sawyer said. "Unless I was missing some context…"

"Janice did seem to have changed," Olivia replied. "She never was one of the bad ones, but she was part of it… So I'm glad she stood up to Eddie. Better late than never for some of these things."

"So what happened exactly?" he asked. "How did this even start?"

Olivia brushed a curl off of her forehead. "There was this bush party. I was never the party-going kind of girl. I mean, if Mom had known I'd even gone, she would have marched out there and dragged me home by my ear. But I lied—said I was sleeping over at Mia's. These guys got frisky with me, and I fought them off, told them to leave me alone. They didn't back off until I actually screamed at them that I'd report them for attempted rape. That stopped them in their tracks, but they were mad. I'd embarrassed them in front of their buddies. And the next day at school, they were all telling these stories about how I'd gone off and done these unspeakable things with them."

"Lying in retaliation," Sawyer said.

"Exactly."

"And people believed it?"

"Something that juicy spreads like wildfire. No one cares if it's true. It made my senior year complete misery. Besides, I was never exactly popular..."

"So this wasn't the first time you were targeted with bullying."

"There was always someone. Isn't that the way school goes? There were always girls who would steal my gym clothes, or call me names. I thought I'd gotten used to it. But when the rumors started senior year—I just couldn't take it anymore."

"And Eddie…was one of the guys from the party?" he asked, his voice carefully controlled. She heard the thrum of a threat in his tone.

"No," she said with a hoarse laugh. "He was just some idiot who heard the stories and figured he might have a chance with me."

"So these rumors—people really latched on to them," Sawyer said. "Didn't your mother go to the principal or anything?"

"Of course. But none of the taunting happened in front of teachers. Bullying is subtle, and it really took a toll on me. But they figured I deserved it. I was being punished for something I'd never even done."

"I'm sorry you went through that."

"I survived."

"Mostly," he said, and he cast her a sad look.

"Mostly," she agreed. "But I had to be strong—Mom worked really hard, my dad was gone, and Brian needed a big sister who had things under control."

"How old was he?" he asked quietly.

"About thirteen," she said.

She'd tried to be tough, to not care, to push her life forward after that last year of high school. But in the end, when she finally escaped, she'd left behind a brother who felt abandoned. Was there any way to have handled that differently? Not while keeping herself in one piece, there wasn't.

"I couldn't wait to get out of here..." She sucked in a wavering breath. "Being picked on changes how you see yourself. Those words slip beneath your skin. And by the time I left for Montana State, I wasn't the woman I wanted to be, the one I knew I could be. But life in the city gave me this new chance to see myself differently. I didn't second-guess every step I took. I wasn't constantly watching over my shoulder for the next person to say something snide. It's like I woke up."

"You deserve that," he said quietly.

"I think so, too." She sighed. "But even so, I'm wondering now if I might have missed the mark with Brian. Obviously, I went wrong somewhere."

"Didn't he know how people were treating you?" he asked.

"He had an idea, but he wasn't in high school yet—he didn't see most of it. By the time he got there, I was gone…but the rumors had stuck around, and he got teased a lot. Our dad left when he was a toddler, and then I left when things got really hard here, and I guess it just impacted him differently. So when he lost his chance at an education, it all just bubbled up."

"Coming back—is it different at all?" Sawyer looked at her hopefully.

"A bit, but not different enough. Like I said, there have already been a couple of tense interactions, and having Eddie talk to me like that…" Olivia licked her lips. "I feel pieces of myself falling away again. And I'm back to looking over my shoulder. I like myself better in Billings. I'm a whole person there."

Sawyer nodded slowly.

"But you were always a step away from that stuff, and I liked that about you," she added. "It's why we became friends to begin with."

"Huh." He smiled. "That and my stellar personality."

"And your taste in old cowboy movies."

"Right."

Olivia felt a smile tug at her lips. "You and Mia were the best of Beaut, Sawyer. You really were."

"Not good enough to keep you around, though," he said.

She sobered. Back then, she'd had to get out of Beaut if she was going to be able to breathe again. And when her two best friends had fallen in love, she'd known that she had to leave. They didn't need a third wheel, and she didn't have anything left to stay for.

"There are some wounds that don't heal," she said quietly. "Even returning, it's like stepping back in time for me. I hate this. I wish I could just ignore idiots like Eddie and move on, but it's not just the guys like him. There's nothing for me here."

"Is everyone that bad?" he asked.

"No, not everyone. Even back in high school there were some nice people who didn't join in on the bullying. But silence doesn't do much in the face of that kind of nastiness."

"Yeah, I can see that..."

"And since I've come back, I saw some of my mom's friends in church and we had a nice chat. There is a woman I went to school with, Lily, who I'd never known terribly well back then who I've been chatting with on Facebook. We started chatting when we both gave our excuses for the five-year reunion. So there are some decent people—like you, Sawyer. But the cruel ones get under my skin. Maybe more than they should, but—"

"Even if you had someone standing up for you?" he asked. "Because I will."

"To how many people, though?" Olivia asked. "It's subtle, Sawyer. It's sidelong looks, knowing smiles, insinuating comments. Are you going to tackle all of those? Because I can't. And I shouldn't have to. I have a life in the city where I'm respected without a fight. In the city, if someone is a jerk, I can cut them out of my life without much effort. It's better for me."

Sawyer nodded slowly. "Yeah, I get it."

It was sweet that he wanted to help, but he wasn't a one-man army. Even a guy as well intentioned as Sawyer couldn't tackle this one.

Bella pushed herself to her feet and wandered toward the slide. She looked up at it for a moment, then started up the rungs. Lizzie rose, too, her hands covered in sand, and she watched her sister. Bella got to the top.

"Sit on your bottom," Olivia called out to her. "Bella, sit down."

Bella lowered herself down to her diapered rump, and then slid slowly down the slide. She stopped halfway down, stuck.

Sawyer chuckled and stood up, headed over. He gave her a nudge, helping her slide down the rest of the way, and Olivia smiled as she watched the sweet scene. She pulled her phone out and took a picture. Then she zoomed in on the girls and took another one. She'd send these to Sawyer—the start of his new memories.

She lowered her phone. Beaut was good for Sawyer—she could see that. It had been good for his little family, good for his future. But it was no longer home for Olivia. It couldn't be. Home was supposed to be safe and secure, where she could let herself exhale.

Lizzie went up the ladder, and Sawyer put a hand out, helping her sit down so she could slide next. He glanced toward Olivia, catching her eye.

"This is about new memories now," he said. "For you, too."

"It wouldn't be a fresh start for me," she said. "I remember."

This town's memory wasn't easily shaken. And a woman could only take so much.

Chapter Eight

That afternoon, Bella fell asleep on the floor next to a stuffed animal, and Sawyer transferred her to her crib. Lizzie was ready to sleep, too, and it only took her a couple of minutes of squirming around to find the right position and her eyes drooped shut.

He looked down at his sleeping daughters in their matching cribs. It had been a long day. But he was starting to notice some differences between the girls—Bella had a quicker temper, and Lizzie was more mischievous. Bella tended to pull the elastics out of her hair, and Lizzie didn't mind hers. Lizzie was obsessed with shoes, and Bella was constantly putting things into her mouth. He and Olivia had fished more than one leaf or pine cone out of her cheek.

He had started a game with himself, watching the girls play or interact, and then guessing which was which. He'd check their hands for the initials that had started to fade now from washing, and he was right more often than not. It felt good. He was figuring stuff out.

Sawyer closed the bedroom door behind him and came out into the living room. He pushed a laundry basket aside so he could sink into the couch. Olivia sat in the rocking chair opposite him, and she shot him a weary smile.

"Thanks for today," she said. "I'm supposed to be helping you remember, not unloading my own issues onto you."

"Hey, that's not true," he said with a shake of his head. "We're friends, and I've got your back, okay?"

"You can't take on a whole town," she reminded him with a low laugh.

204 *A Rancher to Remember*

Couldn't he? As long as Olivia was here, he would protect her. Even after she left, he'd defend her. No one was going to talk badly about her within his hearing.

"Watch me," he muttered.

Sawyer had seen a more vulnerable side to Olivia today, and for the first time, he'd been the one guiding her, supporting her. And he'd liked that. He hadn't liked that she'd been treated that way by that Eddie creep, but he was glad he was there to see it—there to say something, at least. Even if it wasn't enough, she deserved someone defending her.

A car pulled into the drive, and Sawyer and Olivia both turned to look out the living room window. It was a little white hatchback, and when it parked, an older man with gray, receding hair got out. He wore a suit and cowboy boots, but his head was bare.

"Who's that?" Sawyer asked.

"That's your pastor," she replied. "He's the one who married you and Mia. And he officiated her funeral."

"Oh." Sawyer leaned forward to get a better look. "I wonder what he wants."

The pastor seemed to be headed for the front door, so Sawyer walked over to open it before he knocked or rang the bell… Did they have a doorbell? He wasn't sure. He pulled the door open and the older man met him with a smile.

"Sawyer. Good to see you. I heard about your accident and wanted to come by and see how you were."

Sawyer nodded, and stepped back. "Hello."

"Do you remember me at all?"

Sawyer shook his head. "I'm sorry. I don't."

"I'm Pastor Herschel." He put out a hand and shook Sawyer's warmly. "Is this a convenient time?"

"Yeah, sure."

Pastor Herschel came inside, wiped his boots on the mat, and shot a smile in Olivia's direction.

"Good to see you again, Olivia. I thought I saw you in the congregation on Sunday, but I didn't catch you on your way out."

Olivia stood up and shook the pastor's hand. They seemed to know each other rather well, and Sawyer watched them in idle curiosity.

"Where are the girls?" the pastor asked, looking around.

"They're having a nap," Olivia said.

"Oh, so I'll keep it down then." The pastor smiled. "Sawyer, how are you doing? This can't be an easy time for you."

"I'm okay," Sawyer said. "I quite honestly don't really remember much. I remember Mia's funeral a little bit..."

"I was the one who performed the funeral," the pastor said with a solemn nod. "And your wedding."

"Yeah, Olivia just told me that." Sawyer pulled the laundry basket off the couch and put it to the side. "Have a seat."

The older man sat down, and his gaze moved between him and Olivia. "I wanted to see if there is anything I can do to help."

"It'll just take a bit of time," Olivia said.

"He's getting a few memories back, but it's slow."

"That's great. I'm glad to hear it." Pastor Herschel nodded a couple of times. "Can I be honest, son?"

"Yeah, that would be preferable," Sawyer replied.

"You weren't a churchgoer, but your uncle is. I don't want to mislead you here."

"I was told that much," Sawyer said. "What was my problem, then? Because my wife was a churchgoer, right? And my uncle still is... Olivia here seems to be."

"You've been very angry," the old man said. "With God. With church. You didn't want anything to do with us."

"So I wasn't just busy," Sawyer concluded. "A workaholic."

"Well, you made yourself busy." The pastor smiled. "You came to church on Christmas and Easter. You'd promised your wife you'd do that much. And you stared out a window the whole time." The pastor paused.

"You did send the girls to church with Lloyd and your cousin, Ellen."

"I didn't know that…"

"I came here today because your uncle thought I might be able to help. He asked me to come. When your memory comes back, I don't want you to think that I took advantage of your condition. I'm telling you straight— you don't like me much."

"On a personal level?" Sawyer frowned.

"Oh, no, it's not personal. I'm a minister. I stand for things that irritate you. And I don't mind telling you that I've been praying for you by name for years."

"What happened?" Sawyer asked with a frown. "Olivia mentioned that I was pretty anti-church. But why?"

"It was your dad's death," Olivia said quietly, and Sawyer turned toward her. "He passed away when you were only a teenager, and you missed him desperately. You hated the platitudes—you know, when people say that the person has gone to a better place, so we shouldn't be sad, but should be happy for them. That sort of thing. That's where it started. I guess there were a few older folks in the church who tried to take over and give you some guidance after your dad died, and it didn't go well."

"Oh…" Sawyer said, trying to dig back into his mind. But it was no use. He couldn't remember any of this, and when he looked at the weather-worn pastor sitting awkwardly on the couch, he couldn't even pull up any negative feelings. "Well, I guess that's good to know…"

"I've come here today in good faith. I want to be here for you—for whatever you might need," the pastor said slowly. "I understand that when you get your memory back, you'll likely get back a lot of your old feelings towards the church. But right now, while you're trying to remember it all, if there is anything I can do to help you, I want to do it."

Sawyer looked around himself. What did he need? He had his family, and Olivia. He had his girls… There was no pressure for him to get back to work to pay bills since he was living with his uncle. What he needed was his memory, and the pastor couldn't do much about that.

But when he looked over at Olivia sitting on that rocking chair, the sadness in her eyes that nothing seemed to touch… She needed more than just some cowboy telling off the idiots who insulted her—she needed healing of her own.

"There is something," Sawyer said, clearing his throat. "Not for me—but for Olivia."

Olivia's gaze sharpened and she eyed him cautiously.

"Of course," the pastor said. "What can I do?"

"This is all confidential, I presume?" Sawyer said.

"Absolutely."

"She and her brother have been at odds for years, I understand," Sawyer said slowly. "And it's breaking her heart. She misses him a whole lot. If there were something you could do for her—that would mean a great deal to me."

The pastor turned to Olivia, and color bloomed in her cheeks.

"It's private," she said with a quick shake of her head. "He has some strong feelings, and—"

"It's delicate," the pastor said.

"Yes. Very."

"Everyone is a little delicate, Olivia," the pastor said quietly.

Tears misted her eyes. "He doesn't like me much anymore, Pastor. Too much water has passed under the bridge, I guess."

"But he's still your brother," the pastor pressed.

"Yes." Her chin trembled ever so slightly.

"And you want to fix things."

She nodded. "I do. He's not a Christian, though, and he's not likely to respect you as a pastor. Just a warning."

Pastor Herschel nodded twice. "Will you leave it with me? I'll pray on it, and see where the Spirit leads."

"Sure." Olivia looked over at Sawyer, and past the tears in her eyes, he saw gratitude. Well, Sawyer wasn't the only one who needed some help these days.

"Let's pray together..." the pastor said, and he folded his hands.

As the pastor prayed—for reconciliation, for fresh starts, for forgiveness and blessings—Sawyer felt a weight lift off his shoulders.

Lord, I want to be a better man than I was before, he prayed in his heart. *I want to be kinder, more present for my daughters. I want to be the man I should have been. Please, Lord, change me.*

It was time to put all that bitterness that he couldn't even remember into the past and to move forward. Not for himself, so much, as for his little girls.

And then, as he listened to the low voice of the praying pastor, he remembered...

"Thank you so much," Olivia said, standing at the door to see Pastor Herschel off again. Sawyer had slipped away after the prayer, and she wasn't sure where he'd gone.

"I'm glad I got to see you, too," the pastor said, stepping outside.

"I don't know what to say about my brother, though," she said hesitantly. "I didn't mean to make this visit about my own problems. You were supposed to be here for Sawyer."

"He seems more concerned about you right now," the older man said.

"Yes…" Sawyer had been trying to help, and she appreciated it, even if his sweet gesture made him more difficult to hold at arm's length. Being here with Sawyer was already opening up old memories, old feelings… old failures. She felt her eyes mist in spite of her attempt to hold back her emotions. "The thing is, Pastor, this situation with my brother is embarrassing for me. I should be able to sort this out on my own, but somehow it's gotten too big for me to get a handle on."

"All families have their tensions," he said with a kind smile. "As a minister, I see it all. Believe me, this is not so rare as you may think. Deaths in the family have this tendency to be watershed events. Sawyer's father's death, your mother's death… Everything afterward is different. Relationships change, dynamics change. These things do happen. You're not the only ones."

"Mom would have hated this," Olivia admitted, a lump in her throat. "She wanted me to take care of Brian. Instead, we have a mess."

"We'll both pray, and then we'll see how the Lord moves us," the pastor said, reaching out to touch her arm. "And keep taking care of Sawyer. I understand that he doesn't remember any of us, but you being here—it helps more than a pastor popping by. I can tell you that."

"Thanks," she said with a weak shrug. "I hope so."

"Tell Sawyer thank you for letting me visit," the pastor said. "I hope I didn't offend him."

"I'll let him know. It was nice of you to come by."

The pastor waved and headed down the

steps and toward his car. Olivia shut the front door and sucked in a deep breath.

She crossed the living room and looked around. Where had Sawyer gone off to? Down the hallway, the toddlers' bedroom door was open, and she walked softly in that direction.

"Sawyer?"

She peeked inside, and she saw him sitting on an ottoman, elbows resting on his knees, his back to her. The room was dim, the curtains shut, and the sound of the toddlers' soft breathing came from the two cribs across the room. She stepped inside, and when she came closer, she saw that he was holding a tiny pair of socks, sized for newborns, in his hands.

"Sawyer?" she repeated quietly.

He looked up, and there were tears sparkling in his eyes. "I remember it…"

He ran his calloused fingers over the soft cotton.

"You do?" she breathed.

"I remember her belly—Mia's. It was

huge." His voice was low and rough. "I could put my hand on it, and I'd feel them move around in there..." A tear slipped past his lashes, and he dashed it off his face with the heel of his other hand. "And I remember taking them home... They were so tiny. I was so alone. I missed Mia so much. I can't even describe it. Lloyd sat up with me that whole night, and we took turns giving the girls their bottles of formula. Just two guys and two tiny baby girls..."

"Oh, Sawyer..." she breathed.

"I don't remember all of it, but I do remember that," he said huskily. "I remember trying to put diapers on them, and they were so little that the diapers just about fell off of them. And I was afraid to put them into the cribs, because the house was cold—it was wintertime—and I was afraid they'd freeze. So me and Lloyd, we sat up together, each with a baby on our chests, and we kept them warm."

Tears misted Olivia's eyes in response. He

was getting it back…and she could see how much he loved his daughters.

He licked his lips and let out a shaky breath. "Is the pastor gone?"

"I saw him off," Olivia said. "He was worried he'd offended you."

"Nah. I just… I remembered, and I came in here to see them, and to see if I could get more back." He swallowed hard, and turned his watery gaze toward her. "Olivia, I wasn't much of a husband, or a father."

"That's not true——" she started.

"Yeah, it is." He shook his head. "It is. Mia loved me, but I put her through a lot. I didn't talk about my feelings, and I worked constantly. She put up a good front, but I wasn't making her happy."

"I don't believe that," Olivia said fiercely.

"Ask Lloyd. He's the one who filled me in. I wouldn't even go to church with her." He shook his head. "After she died, I sent my daughters to church with extended family. What kind of a father does that?"

"A hurt one," she said quietly. "At least you sent them."

He shook his head. "Not good enough."

Sawyer rose to his feet and walked over to Bella's crib. He reached down and stroked her cheek with the back of his finger. He was motionless for a moment, and Olivia wondered if she should leave him, but then he turned back toward her.

"You didn't know me as well as you think," he said bitterly.

"Sawyer, I don't know what kind of man you think you were, but I knew you!" she said, crossing the room and stopping in front of him. "Family has all sorts of tensions— the pastor was just telling me that. And your family was no exception. But that doesn't change who you are!"

"And who am I?" he asked, spreading his hands. "Because I don't remember enough, and what I've heard isn't great."

One of the toddlers moaned in her sleep, and they both looked toward the crib.

"You're my friend," she said, lowering her

voice to a whisper. She met his gaze, silently begging him to believe her. "You're the guy who could make me laugh when I felt at my worst. You were kind, in little ways other people weren't. You used to get sad when you saw a dead baby bird at the bottom of a tree. And you once carried a newborn calf in your arms for a full mile to get it back to the barn where you could warm it up." She put her hand on his arm.

"I don't remember that..." he murmured.

"Well, I do," she said. "When I was working as a waitress, you saw this old farmer treat me like garbage. He said I messed up his order, and maybe I did. But you came in and made this big scene and left me a twenty-dollar tip in front of everyone." She smiled mistily. "When I got off of work, you wouldn't let me spend the money on ice cream to share. You paid for the ice cream, too."

"I did that?" he asked quietly.

"Yeah, you did. And more. You were my best friend until I had to step back and let your wife be your best friend. But when I did that, I was giving up a really great guy in my life..." Her voice caught. "And I missed you..."

Sawyer raised his hand and touched her cheek. It was only then that she realized a tear had escaped, and she leaned her face into his warm palm.

"I wish I could remember that stuff," he breathed.

"I remember it for the both of us," she said, and a lump rose in her throat.

His dark eyes met hers, and she could see the anguish swimming there. But there was hope now, too, and as his gaze moved over her face, she felt the moment between them deepen. His lips parted, and he stepped closer to her, so that she could feel the warmth of his chest emanating from him. He ran his hands down her arms, and they felt strong and warm against her chilled skin. In their friendship, they'd tried to avoid moments like this—touching each other, holding on to each other…because they knew where it would lead all too easily.

"Why is it that you can make me feel better?" he murmured.

"I'm useful that way," she said, attempting to joke, but it didn't land, and he didn't laugh. He reached up and touched a curl at the side of her face. This time, she refused to lean her cheek into his touch, no matter how much she wanted to.

Sawyer might not remember the simmering chemistry between them, but she did. They'd been friends, but they'd also fought to keep it that way, because without some firm self-control, their relationship would have tumbled into the romantic.

He made her feel better, too. He was still the one she could rely on, even when his memory had betrayed him.

"Sawyer…" she breathed. He should be warned… She'd never told him about this part of their friendship.

But then there was the sound of the side

door opening and the clomp of boots. Lloyd was home, and Olivia took a step back.

She licked her lips and suppressed a sigh.

"Your uncle's here," she said, her voice shaking ever so slightly.

"Yeah." He cleared his throat.

Olivia didn't know what he was feeling, but she knew better than to let herself go with the flow of whatever was building between them again.

"I'm going to work with my uncle this afternoon," Sawyer said briskly.

"Sawyer, you're recovering—" she began, but a searing look from him silenced her.

"I need to do this," he said quietly. "Can you watch my girls?"

His girls… She nodded. "Yes."

"Thank you."

And he brushed past her, out of the bedroom. She could hear his footsteps going down the hall and she shut her eyes.

Lord, keep my feet on the ground, she prayed. *I have to remember for us both.*

Chapter Nine

Sawyer grabbed his jacket and got his hat off the peg by the side door. Lloyd stood at the counter, pouring coffee from the pot into his thermos, steam billowing up in a fragrant cloud. The older man looked over at Sawyer in surprise.

"I'm working with you this afternoon," Sawyer said curtly. "And if you don't like that, I'm going out on my own."

Lloyd didn't answer, just slowly screwed the lid back onto his thermos.

"So, are you driving, or am I?" Sawyer asked.

Lloyd met his gaze seriously. "What happened?"

An image of Olivia was still vivid in his mind—her upturned face, her teary eyes, and the way his heart had thudded in his ears as he looked down at her. He'd wanted more—to hold her again, to pull her closer... He pushed it back.

"Nothing. Apparently, I'm a bit of a workaholic. The accident didn't change that."

"Was hoping it might," Lloyd muttered, and then he sighed. "Fine. I'll drive."

Sawyer had expected a bigger fight from his uncle, but maybe the old guy had seen it coming. Sawyer headed outside, letting the screen door slam shut behind him, and he stood in the cool breeze, his thoughts spinning.

He'd almost kissed Olivia. If Lloyd hadn't come back, he probably would have. There had been something about that cozy quiet of the room, her deep belief in his goodness, and those sparkling brown eyes that pulled him in so easily... And even now, all he could think about was covering her soft pink lips with his.

Having her in his arms would be a powerful comfort right about now. But he hardly remembered his own history. He had no business starting up a romantic relationship. He didn't even know who he was yet! Besides, she wasn't sticking around—she'd made that clear. And he understood why.

Sawyer had to get out and work today, though, for his own sanity and to give himself some distance from Olivia. Whatever he was feeling for her was strong and confusing. She was supposed to be a friend— wasn't that what she'd told him? They'd been buddies. Obviously, he was overcompensating for his memory loss, and he could only imagine how offended she'd be once she had a minute to think this all through.

When he got himself sorted out this afternoon, he'd be able to focus on what mattered—put the hard work into becoming the man he needed to be for his kids. Maybe his workaholic tendencies wouldn't be such a liability after all, if he could just refocus his energy. He wouldn't let his daughters grow up resentful. He'd make sure they got what they needed, and then some.

The door to the house opened behind him, and Sawyer glanced back to see Lloyd come outside with his thermos in one hand and a sandwich in the other. He took a big bite of the sandwich, then nodded to the truck.

"On second thought, you drive," Lloyd said past the food in his mouth. "I'll tell you where to go."

Sawyer climbed in on the driver's side.

"The key's on the visor," Lloyd said, swallowing. "And you do what I say when I say it. You hear? I don't want another accident on my hands with you."

"Got it." Sawyer flicked down the visor and caught the key as it dropped. He started the truck and with the rumbling beneath him, he felt a wave of relief.

This must have been what it felt like to head out for a day on the ranch. If he needed some comfort today, he'd get it the old-fashioned way—with hard work. He couldn't dump his emotions onto Olivia.

* * *

That evening when Sawyer and Lloyd got back, he was tired and it felt good. A lot of the work was starting to come back to him. He still needed Lloyd to prompt him with what to do, but his muscles seemed to remember the movements, and he was catching on quickly. Some of it was just logic—usually what he thought he should do next considering everything going on around him turned out to be the right thing. He was going to be able to pitch in around here a little bit more, and that was a relief.

When they got back for dinner, Olivia had already cooked. It was some sort of meat sauce on top of rice. It was new to him, but it tasted good, especially as tired and hungry as he was. Olivia fed the girls some rice and pieces of meat without the sauce. They didn't eat much of it, and Lloyd grabbed them some yogurt and crackers—those disappeared a lot faster.

Sawyer had missed the girls while he was gone. He was kind of relieved to feel that pang. He'd been half afraid he wouldn't, and didn't know what that would say about him. So after dinner, he cuddled his daughters on his lap and read them a story until they nodded off.

"Did you need a hand?" Olivia asked.

"I can do it," Lloyd said, coming into the living room. "I've kind of missed this part."

"Oh...of course." Olivia smiled and sank back into her spot on the couch.

Lloyd eased Bella off Sawyer's lap and Sawyer hoisted up Lizzie. They ambled down the hall together, and Sawyer glanced back once to see Olivia watching them with a tender look on her face. Then they headed into the bedroom and the men lowered the toddlers into their cribs. Lizzie moaned a little as she was getting resettled, but it only took a few seconds for both girls to be snoring softly from their beds. Sawyer closed the curtains, and Lloyd shot Sawyer a smile as they both headed for the door.

This must have been the routine before Olivia arrived, he realized, him and Lloyd pitching in together with the kids. Lloyd seemed to know the drill.

"Back to normal," Lloyd said. "Almost."

"Yeah?" Sawyer wished he could remember that.

"We held down the fort," Lloyd said, and then he nodded down the hall. "I'm turning in, too."

"All right." Sawyer nodded. "Good night."

He headed back out to the living room, and he found Olivia where he'd left her, sitting on the side of the couch, her legs tucked up underneath her. He paused, gave her an uncertain smile. She looked sweet and soft, and he cleared his throat, gazing down at his boots instead.

"About before..." he said.

"We don't have to talk about it," she said.

"You're trying to be nice, but I think we do," he said. "I know it got kind of...intense earlier. And I know that's on me. I'm starting over in a lot of ways, and I don't remember much of anything between us, so I guess I'm making a fool of myself. And I'm sorry."

"You're no fool," she said, her voice low. That same certainty was back on her face from earlier, and he wished he could believe her.

"I'm a bit of one," he said ruefully. "Maybe I'm just lonely or something, but I'm finding myself slipping into... I don't know."

He didn't want to confess any of this, but he couldn't very well go on with some awkward moment standing between them, either. She was the only friend he had right now—that he could remember.

"It's funny," she said quietly. "I thought it would be different this time. But we always did have this problem."

He sank down onto the other end of the couch, his gaze locked on her. "You told me we were friends."

"And we were," she said with a nod. "We chose to be friends because it wouldn't work between us to be more... I honestly thought that the chemistry would be gone between us by now."

"So we were always like this?" he asked,

shaking his head. "The attraction, I mean. Because I know I feel it and I was beating myself up all afternoon thinking that I'd probably offended you."

"No, you didn't offend me," she said, then shrugged weakly.

"Good..." He let out a breath of relief. "But I'm still sorry. I've been dreading bringing it up with you, but I know I have to. Just to clear the air, I guess. I shouldn't have let myself—"

"Sawyer," she interrupted him. "We knew better than to toy with these kinds of feelings. So...we made a pact."

"What sort?" he asked.

"To keep things strictly friendly. No romance. No romantic settings. No hand holding or hugging, or...anything that would make our decision harder to stick to."

It all started to make more sense now...the distance between them when they'd needed each other most.

"Ah... No hugging. Even in the hardest of times."

"Yes," she said, and tears misted her eyes. "Even when it broke our hearts. No hugging."

"Okay." He eyed her uncertainly. "So, what's happening now?"

"I guess it wasn't just about a shared history," she said.

Sawyer let out a long breath. "I can't... I mean, I shouldn't—" He winced. "I need to be a good dad, Olivia. I don't think any of it comes to me real naturally, but I'm determined to do better by my girls now than I did in the past."

She was silent and dropped her gaze to her lap.

"I know I started something earlier today, and I'm sorry about it. I've got to get myself straightened out, and starting up a romance when I don't even remember who I am—"

"Sawyer, you don't have to explain," she said quickly. "It's the same for me. I can't just reverse course and come back to Beaut. I wasn't happy here, and I'm not willing to fight idiots like Eddie for the rest of my life. I know what I need, too."

"And it isn't this." He waggled his finger between them.

"No, it isn't." She smiled sadly. "We've had this conversation before. You just don't remember it."

"Right." He nodded.

"And for the record, we had no trouble with our attraction to each other during your marriage. You were in love. You only had eyes for her. I promise you that."

That did help. "So how do we handle this, then?"

"We…um…follow our rules."

"No hugging. No touching. No romantic anything," he said.

He could still remember that isolated scene in his head—Olivia in the dark jacket, her eyes filled with anguish and his longing to hold her… The memory was so stark that it still sent a shiver through him.

Hard work. That's what had worked for them in the past to clear his head, and they'd come out the other side okay, it would seem. It was his plan for being a better dad, too. No one could fault him on his work ethic. This time, he'd apply it to the right things.

"I won't do that again," he said. "I'll keep my hands to myself."

"Me, too," she said, then laughed softly. "We'll get our balance back. I promise."

"I'm just going to do the dishes," he said. "You turn in or whatever you want with your evening."

"Do you need a hand?" she asked.

More time with her wasn't going to help this. Not tonight.

"Nah. I'm fine," he said.

"Okay, well…" She smiled hesitantly. "Good night, I guess."

"Good night." He met her gaze once more, and she looked so soft and gentle that turning and walking away was harder than it should have been. But he was glad they'd cleared this up. Doing the dishes would give him a chance to think by himself, to shake that image of her upturned face out his head and get himself back on track.

She was here to help him remember, and she was doing that. Whatever was tumbling around in his heart wasn't her problem.

Olivia lay on her bed that night, long past the time she heard the gentle clatter from the kitchen go silent. The house was quiet, and her mind was still reeling. Why couldn't things be easier with Sawyer? She'd truly thought that their chemistry would be different if he didn't remember her. They'd become friends under such odd circumstances that she'd often thought if they'd met at a different time, they'd have politely nodded and walked in different directions. It was the strange timing—her loneliness, and one quiet evening at the diner where she was working.

When she told Mia about meeting Sawyer and how he'd suggested that cowboy movie marathon, Mia had encouraged her to go.

"So what if it is a date?" Mia had said with

a laugh. "Is that so bad? If I stumbled across a cute cowboy asking me out, I'd be going."

When Sawyer dropped her off at home that night, he had kissed her cheek. It was sweet—but she'd known it couldn't go anywhere, and she knew that her heart couldn't take a fling. She wasn't the kind of girl who recovered that quickly when her emotions were involved. So she made it clear.

It had seemed so easy and logical then. When it started to seem like she might fall for Sawyer in spite of all the reasons not to, Olivia invited Mia along for one of their movie dates, just to ensure things stayed strictly friendly between them.

And the rest was history.

So why was that chemistry charging between them again? Was it just more odd circumstances pushing them together? They were both a little vulnerable right now. Why was it that that they couldn't seem to come back into each other's lives when they were both doing just fine? Was Sawyer her crutch in times of need? Very likely—she could admit it.

Sawyer's current attraction to her could be explained—he was lonely, and he couldn't remember any other women. Give him options and maybe it would lessen. It sure worked when Mia was in the picture.

But her feelings for him…she knew better. Or she should, at least. Why was she letting herself soften up toward him? He belonged in Beaut. And even if she wanted to come back—which she didn't—she couldn't afford to. The city hospital paid better, and she needed the money now more than ever.

She needed her own emotional equilibrium more than ever, too.

As she lay on the bed, flicking through the pictures on her phone, she looked down at those two sweet little faces. His daughters were adorable, and she'd managed to snap one picture of Sawyer looking down at them as they chattered up at him in baby talk. His expression was so endearingly baffled that she couldn't help but laugh.

Olivia knew all the reasons she didn't belong here, but it was getting harder and harder to disentangle them from her real reason for being here—she was supposed to be orchestrating a reconciliation.

She heaved a sigh. This was no random meeting between the two of them. She'd come on a mission.

As if on cue, her phone rang, the sound loud and jarring in the silence, and she picked up hurriedly, not wanting to wake anyone else up. It was the Whites' phone number.

"Hello?" she said softly.

"Olivia." It was Wyatt this time. "How are you doing?"

He sounded official, professional. A little bit daunting. This was his senatorial voice—the one that got results, no doubt.

"I'm fine," she said. "How are you?"

"We're good. Just checking in. We haven't heard from you in a few days."

Olivia sighed. "Senator, it isn't so simple."

"It never is. But we have a deal, don't we?"

"I need more time," she said. "I'm doing my best."

"What could possibly be standing in your way?" he asked with a sigh. "You're in Beaut, and you've seen Sawyer, you say. Either he's willing to see us, or he isn't. Which is it?"

"I haven't brought it up yet," she admitted. "He's had an accident and he's still recovering."

"Is he in the hospital? Is he unable to care for the girls?" She could see where his mind was jumping with that.

"No!" she said with a sigh. "It's not like that—"

"But he's fragile enough that you don't want to upset him, I presume?"

She'd have to provide some sort of answer. She hated this feeling of having explain her time here. But she'd come for them, and there was no getting around it.

"He's physically capable of caring for his children," she said firmly. "I can vouch for that as a nurse. But his accident affected his memory. It's not permanent, but he needs a bit more time to remember you properly so I can bring reconciliation up. He isn't quite there yet."

That should buy her a bit more time, shouldn't it? It was the truth, after all.

"So he doesn't remember us…"

"Not fully," she hedged. "He won't be able to make a decision about you one way or the other until he's fully healed. And that will be soon, I'm sure. He's been recovering very well so far."

"We should come down—" Wyatt said.

"No!" she said. "Look, he's still the same old Sawyer. He's not about to be bullied into anything. And I won't be part of that. You asked me to help you reconcile, and that's what I'm committing to doing. Fairly. And honestly."

There was silence on the other end for a moment, and then Irene came on the line.

"What about my granddaughters?" she asked, and Olivia heard tears in her voice.

"They're doing just fine," Olivia assured her. "They're happy and sweet and full of energy."

"Could you send me a picture of them?" Irene asked. "Just to tide us over. We'll wait a bit longer, but a picture would help."

If it would keep the Whites at bay for a little while, would it hurt to send a picture? These were their granddaughters, after all, and heavy-handed as they were, all they wanted was to be in the girls' lives. She paused, considering.

"Please," Wyatt added, and the old bluster was gone from his voice. "For Mia."

Olivia's heart softened at the mention of her friend and she sighed.

"Hold on."

She pulled her phone away from her face, selected a picture of the toddlers together, staring bright-eyed into the camera. Then she sent it to Irene's number.

"I've sent a picture to Irene," she said. "That's Bella and Lizzie."

"Oooooh..." Irene sighed. "They're precious. Aren't they sweet, Wyatt?"

"Yeah, they're pretty cute," Wyatt said

gruffly. "I can see Mia in those cheeks. She had the chubbiest cheeks at that age, remember?"

"She sure did…" Irene's voice was soft.

"Thank you, Olivia," Wyatt said. "Truly. From the bottom of our hearts. We look forward to hearing from you."

"My pleasure," she said. "Good night, sir."

As she hung up the phone, she heaved a quiet sigh. Sawyer did have family out there—more than his uncle and a few cousins. He had Mia's parents, too. And they wanted to be a part of his life. She'd gotten sidetracked with her own feelings toward the man, but she'd come to help mend a fractured family. Her motives had been pure.

And if she could help this family, then the Whites would help hers…

It was time to talk to Sawyer about his in-laws. It would be nice to have had a bit more time for him to recover, but now that she'd sent a picture of his daughters to their grandparents, she should tell him that Mia's parents wanted a relationship.

He couldn't remember them, and in the interest of a reconciliation, that might be for the best. But she couldn't hold this back any longer. Sawyer needed to know about them. Tomorrow morning, she'd make it right.

Chapter Ten

Sawyer put a pot of oatmeal onto a cork pad in the center of the table. Lloyd stood at the sink, scrubbing his hands as he always did when he came back from the barn. In the last few days, this scene had become a bit of a routine for them. A nice routine—comforting. Funny how fast these things could take root.

This morning when Sawyer read his Bible, he came across another passage he'd underlined in Second Corinthians, and it had been rattling around in his head ever since.

Therefore if any man be in Christ, he is a new creature: old things are passed away; behold, all things are become new.

Sawyer hadn't had a lot of choice in his restart, but he still found comfort in those words. The problem for him was that he couldn't remember his old mistakes. On the surface, that was a blessing. Who didn't want to put their mistakes so far behind them that they didn't even remember them? But if a man couldn't remember his mistakes, how could he learn from them and keep himself from repeating them a second time?

The pastor had said he'd been angry. Bitter. Sawyer sighed. With the return of his memory, would he also get that baggage back, too? That had been preoccupying his thoughts.

"The pastor came by yesterday," Sawyer said, and Lloyd grabbed a towel to dry his hands and turned.

"Yeah?" He saw the trepidation in his uncle's eyes.

"It's okay," Sawyer said. "It was kind of him to drop in."

"Good..." Lloyd nodded quickly. "Real good. So, did he help at all?"

"A bit," he replied. "He actually filled me in on something. He said I was pretty angry with the church and all that."

"Oh, yes…"

"Why didn't you tell me?" Sawyer shook his head. "You said I was just a workaholic."

"If you didn't remember it, why drag it up?" Lloyd said. "Maybe you'd be able to just move on."

Sawyer sighed. "How much more are you hiding from me?"

Lloyd grabbed some bowls from the cupboard and put them on the table. His movements were casual and relaxed, but his jaw had gotten tight. Then he looked up at Sawyer. "Every story has a hundred different sides."

"My story, you mean?" Sawyer pressed.

"Everyone's story," Lloyd replied. "It all depends on how you tell it. A man's personal history is written by whoever feels like talking about him. I'd rather you write your own."

"I can't remember it," Sawyer retorted. "How can I?"

Lloyd nodded slowly. "Sawyer, I've done things I wish I could forget. I've held onto stupid ideas that I wish I hadn't. There was about a decade when I was furious with women. I blamed them for not seeing what I had to offer, and I was a real jerk. I was single, bitter and lonely, and I figured women were to blame for that. It embarrasses me now. And I only tell you about it because you'll remember it eventually anyway. But people do change. They do grow. And if I could have my outlook right now and forget a few of those embarrassing details from the past, I'd do it. So who am I to drag up your past mistakes?"

Lloyd met Sawyer's gaze earnestly, then he pulled out his chair with a scrape and sat down. He reached for the pot of oatmeal and dished himself up a hearty portion.

"But would you be who you are today without having learned a few things the hard way?" Sawyer asked. "If you can't remember how you've grown…a man might go backward."

"You haven't," Lloyd replied. "And I told you what you needed to know—that you used to work too hard. That's what you did with all your frustration and hard feelings. The rest… Son, when we ask for forgiveness, God throws our sins into the darkest part of the sea. No need to go fishing for them."

His uncle meant well, but Sawyer needed more than blissful oblivion. He needed to know who he was—as a full person. That was going to include some uncomfortable stuff, but how could he move forward without it?

"Speaking of making a few changes in my own life," Lloyd said, dropping his gaze. "I have a guest coming this morning. She's… she's interested in the calving, and I figured I'd show her a few things firsthand."

"She?" Sawyer raised an eyebrow and shot his uncle a grin.

"You saw her at the church—Evelyn. I was talking to her by the truck before we left."

The beautiful brunette. She was interested in calving? Sawyer squinted. "Really?"

"What?" Lloyd chewed the side of his cheek. "She's from the city, and she's never seen the process before. We've done some talking since church."

"Like...on the phone?" Sawyer asked.

"Yes." Lloyd pressed his lips together. "She's a nice woman. I like her. And she's coming by this morning."

"Wow." Sawyer nodded. "Yesterday you would hardly let me touch anything. I slung some bales. But you'll take a complete newbie out there?"

"She's a complete newbie who will stay in the truck if I tell her to," Lloyd snapped. "You don't take orders quite so well."

A teasing smile tugging at his lips. "But I feel the slight, I gotta say."

He was mostly joking, because he did understand exactly why his uncle was willing to bring this woman with him out into the fields—she was stunning. And Lloyd, as he'd explained before, was ready for a woman in his life. That was something Sawyer could sympathize with.

Olivia appeared in the doorway, a toddler on each hip, and she smiled tiredly at them.

"Good morning," she said. "The girls are up."

There was something rather endearing about seeing her like that—in jeans and a white blouse, no makeup and her hair still looking a bit mussed. Lloyd was ready for some female companionship, and Sawyer had to admit that he felt the lack of it, too, when faced with Olivia like this.

Sawyer pushed his chair back out and stood up.

"Thanks for getting them ready," he said. "I didn't hear them. You hungry?"

"Hmm," she replied and stifled a yawn as he took Lizzie out of her arms. He planted a kiss on top of the toddler's curly head, then put her into one of the high chairs. Olivia put Bella into the other one, and he reached over to tweak Bella's plump cheek.

The next couple of minutes were spent

getting oatmeal into the toddler's bowls—
although most of it would end up on themselves and the floor. And once they were all
seated again, he shot Olivia a smile.

"I have to talk to you about something,"
Olivia said as Sawyer passed her a bowl
filled with oatmeal.

"Yeah?" Her expression was serious, and
he sobered. "What's going on?"

"I haven't wanted to bring this up until you
could remember more," she said. "But I don't
think it's right to wait any longer."

She looked hesitantly toward Lloyd.

"Do you need me to—" Lloyd started to
stand.

"No, actually, you might be able to help me
with this," Olivia replied. "It's about Mia's
parents, Irene and Wyatt."

"Okay." Sawyer waited.

"They want to see you."

"Now?" he asked with a shake of his head.

"Not exactly. It's a little bit complicated,"
she went on.

"They thought I wasn't good enough for her," Sawyer said. "Lloyd told me that much."

"Right." She nodded.

"What else did they do?" he asked.

"The Whites are a proud lot," Lloyd said. "They fancy themselves a step above us regular folks. Wyatt's a senator now, and Irene came from money to begin with. They lived here in Beaut while Wyatt was starting his political career so he could get support from some rich ranchers out here."

"But a rancher without a whole lot of cash—" Sawyer said. "Like me—"

"You weren't their plan for their daughter," Olivia confirmed. "And Mia had always been a cooperative girl, doing whatever they asked of her. She was the perfect politician's daughter—beautiful, smart and obedient."

"Until I came along, I take it," he said.

"Yes." Olivia sighed. "Mia fell for you right away. She was smitten. And you encouraged her to be her own woman."

"Not a bad thing," Sawyer said.

"She was taking a year off before college,

and they'd grudgingly gone along with that, but when you asked her to marry you, she gave up a placement at Yale."

"So they were angry," Sawyer said.

"Furious, more like," Lloyd replied. "They told her to pack up and go to school. She'd earned that position at Yale—she was brilliant. You asked her to stay. She married you and told her parents that it was her life. There was an ugly fight, and they told her she was on her own until she decided to come to her senses and leave you."

Sawyer stayed silent, his heart hammering in his chest. Even hearing about it second-hand was infuriating. He stabbed his spoon into his bowl a couple of times, then pushed it away.

"I take it they made good on that offer to leave us alone?" Sawyer said after a moment.

Olivia nodded. "I told you before that they didn't know Mia was pregnant. And when she died in the delivery, they were upset and lashed out—"

"Yeah, you told me about that part," he

said curtly. "So why do they want to see me now?"

Silence descended around the table, and Olivia looked up at him apologetically. "They have granddaughters. It changes things. They realize that they were wrong to push Mia away...and you, of course...and they want to make things right."

"How?" Sawyer demanded.

Olivia blinked. "I don't know, exactly. But they told me they want to talk to you. Reconcile. Get to know Lizzie and Bella a little bit. If you'd let them. They're wealthy people. I'm sure they could help out financially and—"

"I don't need their money," he said, trying to cap that rising worry inside of him. "I work—and I'll work as much as I have to. Lloyd and I have done okay so far. Haven't we?"

"We make ends meet," Lloyd agreed. "And those girls are well loved."

"It isn't really about money," Olivia said. "They're family, Sawyer."

So far, he hadn't heard anything good about these people, and now Olivia wanted him to sit down and talk to them. Without his proper memory. Without knowing what he was dealing with. He felt at a complete disadvantage.

"Tell me something," Sawyer said. "You said before that I was a good man. Were you telling me the truth?"

"Of course!" She leaned forward. "You always were."

"Was I the kind of man who would keep my children away from their grandparents for spite?" He hesitated, because he cared about this answer. It would tell him something he needed to know about himself. "You've said I was angry. Was I mean like that, too?"

Olivia shook her head. "No. You aren't a mean man. You never were. And when you were angry about stuff, you dealt with it on your own and never took it out on other people."

"Lloyd?" Sawyer asked.

"I agree with Olivia," his uncle replied.

"So I wasn't a petty man who would hold my children from their grandparents because of a personal grudge," he said. "But I might have had other reasons to stand back, reasons I didn't tell you about."

Olivia was silent.

"Did they try to contact me after the funeral?" he asked, turning to his uncle.

"A couple of times," Lloyd replied. "You didn't want to sit down with them."

"I was too angry?" Sawyer asked.

"You were mad," Lloyd confirmed. "But it was more than that. You didn't trust them. You felt uncomfortable. You got a bad feeling."

What did his gut tell him now? He wasn't sure. He said a silent prayer for guidance, but no answer seemed to come. He looked over at his daughters, their hands in their oatmeal bowls, and he wondered what was best for them. He was at a complete disadvantage here. If he'd had a lengthy fight with these people, that wasn't good for his girls.

But he'd had a gut instinct back then that had warned him off.

"What would you do?" he asked Lloyd.

"I don't know..." Lloyd shrugged helplessly.

"And you say that they just want to make up?" Sawyer asked Olivia.

"Yes! That's what they're telling me. And I've known them a long time. They can be frustrating, but they loved their daughter. They care about their granddaughters without even knowing them. It's possible to make mistakes and learn from them. People do grow."

Lloyd had just said the same thing this morning, but this seemed a little sudden. If he'd ever heard something good about the Whites, it might be different, but so far, he hadn't. Was he just clinging to past mistakes now, or was he being smart? He had no idea.

Lord, forgive me if I'm wrong.

"I don't want to see them," Sawyer said slowly. "Not yet. I know there's some virtue in forgetting your past mistakes—and even the mistakes of others—but there's some danger there, too. I'm not saying I'll never talk to them. I'm just saying…not yet."

And he felt better with that answer. He wasn't ready. He didn't remember enough, and as these girls' dad, it was his job to do right by them. He wasn't taking that duty lightly.

He'd said no. Olivia sucked in a deep breath. It was his right, and she didn't blame him at this point. But she had been hoping for a different answer. Maybe an agreement just to sit down together, a conversation with the people… That would have been the kind of answer that would have satisfied the Whites. But this answer wasn't going to make them happy…

"Okay, that's understandable," she said slowly. "I'll tell them that."

"Good." Sawyer's expression was more cautious, though. Less open. And she wondered what he was thinking right now.

Olivia had been right that he needed more

time to get his memory back before he could grapple with this issue. But an "I told you so" wouldn't be helpful right now, either. The Whites had been pushing her for answers, and now they would have one. But it wasn't the kind of answer that would prompt the grateful intervention with a hospital board, either.

Except, this wasn't about money—wasn't that what she'd just told Sawyer? This was about a family in pieces that needed to heal. But she'd done more than just talk with the Whites last night…and her stomach sank at the memory. She'd texted them a photo.

It had been going too far. She felt that even more keenly this morning than she had last night, and she licked her lips, wishing she didn't have to confess this part.

"I—" She winced. "Sawyer, I did something you might not like too much…"

"Oh?" He eyed her cautiously. "What's that?"

"Last night, I was talking with Mia's parents. They called me, for the record. They wanted me to put in a good word for them with you. Anyway, I sent them a photo of the girls. I took a couple at the park in town, and they were so cute. When Irene and Wyatt asked for a picture of the girls, I sent one."

Sawyer was silent for a moment, and she watched his face, trying to decode his emotions. But his expression was granite.

"I'm sorry," she added. "I realized after I'd done it that it was overstepping and I didn't have the right. They aren't my kids. I know I was wrong, but I wanted to tell you."

"Yeah, I wish you hadn't done that," he said with a sigh. "But…whatever. It's just a picture, and like you say—they are family, right?"

"They are," she agreed.

"No more of that, though," he said, catching her gaze and holding it. "Not without asking me first."

He was their father, and she could feel that authority in his gaze.

"I promise," she said with a nod.

"Okay. If they want to know about me or the kids, let me be the one who talks to them. And I'll do that when I'm ready."

"That's fair," she agreed.

"You can tell them that."

She wasn't sure what she'd been expecting when coming out here. But now she was hoping that the Whites would still value her contribution here enough to hold up their end of the bargain. She'd been so fixated on how they could help her, that she hadn't fully thought through what she was supposed to achieve. Was delivering a message really worth that much to them? Or were they expecting more of her?

Olivia took a spoonful of sugar and sprinkled it over her oatmeal. The worst was out of the way, and at least she wouldn't have a deception on her conscience. However things worked out with the Whites, she couldn't sacrifice Sawyer in the process.

"So, about Evelyn," Sawyer said, turning to Lloyd. "Is this…romantic yet?"

Olivia flicked her gaze to the older man,

relieved that the topic hand changed, but also interested. Did Lloyd have a girlfriend?

"I'm not sure," Lloyd said, and his tone was carefully controlled.

"Well, what did she say?" Sawyer asked.

"She said she'd love to see my ranch and that the calving season sounding really interesting. She'd never seen a calf born before."

"But how did she say it?" Sawyer asked.

"She put her hand on my arm," Lloyd said. "And she smiled real nice. You were watching us talk. I don't know! What did it look like?"

Olivia couldn't help but smile, too—was this really how men talked when it came to women? They weren't so much different, were they?

Her cell phone rang, and Olivia pulled her phone out of her pocket, meaning to just silence the ringer, but it was her brother's number. Olivia stood up, picking up the call and moving across the kitchen so not to interrupt Sawyer and Lloyd's conversation.

"Brian?" she said.

"Hey." His voice was terse. "So, something's happened."

"What is it?" she asked, her heartbeat speeding up. She put her hand over her other ear to hear him better.

"Shari's parents just found out that she's pregnant, and it's a mess."

"What's going on?" she asked. "I mean, she's a grown woman—"

"Yeah, but they're furious. They want her to move home to have the baby."

"And not marry you..." Olivia concluded.

"So it would seem." Brian sounded angry. In the background she heard a woman's voice, but couldn't make out the words. "Shari's really upset. She's close with her parents, and—"

"What can I do to help?" Olivia asked.

"How'd you like to be a witness at a shotgun wedding?" he asked.

"You're serious?" she asked quietly.

"Well, first of all, I was hoping we could just sit down and talk it all through. I mean, if you can get that debt reduction that you were promised—"

But it wasn't quite so simple as that anymore. Maybe it never was.

"I can't guarantee that, Brian," she said quietly. "I don't think I can deliver what the Whites want. So we might have to give up hope of that offer. But that doesn't mean you don't have options, okay? Let's get together and talk. I might be able to see a solution where you can't right now. What matters is that you two love each other, right?"

"Yeah, right."

"Where are you?" she asked.

"At my place. Shari's on the phone with her dad right now—" The woman's voice rose a little louder, and it sounded like it was an emotional conversation. "Why don't we meet up in town. Say, at the Mug of Mocha. If nothing else, it might help to have someone to talk it out with who isn't screaming at us."

"I can offer that," she said with a low laugh. "No hollering."

"Shari appreciates that you were happy

when you found out," he said. "And… I appreciate that, too. We haven't gotten a lot of congratulations yet."

"I'm sorry," she said. "But I am happy for you. You've got me, at least."

And her little brother was calling her when he was in a bind. That meant more to her than he probably realized. She was Brian's family, after all—the last he had left in this state, at least.

"Can you come now?" Brian asked. "Be there in say, an hour?"

Olivia looked up to find Sawyer and Lloyd staring at her. The toddlers were still playing with their food, but the men were watching her in open curiosity, their own conversation seemingly forgotten.

"Let's say yes, and if that changes, I'll call you," she said.

"Fair enough," her brother replied. "See you soon. I hope."

Olivia hung up the call and tucked her phone away. She smiled hesitantly. "That was Brian," she said. "And things have gotten complicated for him."

"How so?" Sawyer asked.

"His girlfriend's family have just found out that she's pregnant." Olivia licked her lips. "And they're against the idea of those two getting married."

"Sounds familiar," Sawyer said. "Minus the pregnancy." He frowned, looking over at Lloyd. "Right?"

"Right." Lloyd nodded.

"I said I'd go down and talk with Brian and his girlfriend. They just need a sounding board, I think—someone who's actually happy about their baby on the way. Did you want to come with me?" she asked Sawyer. "Maybe another male perspective would help out. I'm not sure what to expect, though."

Sawyer looked toward his uncle.

"I can take a couple of hours with the girls," Lloyd offered. "Evelyn might even like it."

Sawyer was silent for a beat, then nodded.

"Yeah, sure. I can come along," Sawyer said.

"Thank you." Olivia shot him a relieved smile. "Because I have no easy answers for these two. So say a prayer for us, Lloyd. We're going to need it."

Chapter Eleven

Looking around town, Sawyer had started to feel a vague sense of nostalgia for a history he couldn't quite recall. It was a step forward. Mug of Mocha was a small coffee shop in downtown Beaut, with a few tables on a patio outside where a couple of older guys sat, paper coffee cups in front of them, and dogs lying at their feet. Sawyer held the door for Olivia, and she went inside first. He had no idea what to expect here today. He'd come to be a support for Olivia, not because he was some wellspring of wisdom when it came to young love. He couldn't remember his own.

Once inside, Olivia headed for a table at the back where a young cowboy Sawyer recognized from Sunday at church sat with his hat on the table, his hair mussed. The young woman next to him looked wan and a bit scared.

"Hi," Olivia said, sliding onto the bench opposite them. "This is Sawyer. Sawyer, this is Shari."

Sawyer and Shari exchanged smiles. There was a brief round of greetings, and then Olivia reached out and put a hand over Shari's.

"How are you, though, Shari?" Olivia asked quietly. "You look like it's been tough."

"It has been." Shari's eyes welled, and she dabbed at them with a crumpled tissue.

"How far along are you now?" Olivia asked.

"Three months," Shari said. She dropped her gaze.

"How did your family find out?" Olivia asked.

"I…told them." Shari swallowed. "I don't know… It's a big secret to keep, and I told my mom. I'm having a baby…it's huge. I wanted her support, I guess. I knew she'd be upset, but I didn't expect that much disappointment. Or anger."

Sawyer glanced toward Brian. The young man sat silent.

"How long have you been together now?" Sawyer asked him.

"Six months," Brian said.

"Well, seven if you count when you first held my hand—" Shari added.

"Yeah, okay, seven months, I guess."

The young couple exchanged a bashful smile. Seven months. It wasn't really long, and here they were expecting a child together. He could remember the birth of his own girls now, and it was not only a traumatic event, but it was the kind of thing that made a man. Granted, his introduction to fatherhood was more intense because he'd lost his wife at the same time, but being a father—even without his memory—had grounded him and given him a sense of responsibility. Nothing was about him any-more—it was now about his little girls.

Olivia scooted along the bench closer to Shari, and Sawyer leaned his elbows on the table, watching the women talk in lowered voices.

"Hey, man," Brian said with a nod. "How're *you* feeling?"

"Not bad," Sawyer said with a wan smile. "Remembering more every day, so…"

"You don't remember me yet, huh?" Brian asked with a small smile.

"It'll come back," Sawyer said with a shrug. He hated this—admitting how limited he was right now. But a few more memories were surfacing—conversations while riding herd, the way the land rolled out in front of him when he was on horseback surrounded by slowly moving cattle, and the smell of the countryside in high summer.

He'd also started to remember Mia last night. Not huge things, but the way she'd laugh or this really flat look in her eyes when she was good and mad. Apparently, he'd managed to make her mad often enough for that look to be a memory that surfaced before her laughter had. He was still glad to remember it. His life was coming back to him in teaspoon measurements—enough that he could recognize just how inexperienced these two were.

"So, what are you going to do?" Sawyer asked.

Brian cracked his knuckles and frowned, but didn't say anything.

"Because the way I see it, you love this woman. And you're going to be a dad. So are you going to marry her or not?"

"It's complicated," Brian said. "It's not as simple as just getting married anymore."

"My parents are really angry," Shari interjected. "They don't want us getting married at all. Or at least, not yet. They say that we should date another year or two, and then make that kind of decision."

"A little late if there's a baby already on the way," Sawyer said.

"What do *you* want?" Olivia asked, fixing her gaze on the young woman.

"I want my parents to stop hating me," she said, dabbing at her eyes again with that tissue.

"I'm sure they don't hate you," Olivia said, and she passed Shari a napkin. "But are you willing to do what they want to calm them down? To move home, let them help you get ready for the baby, and just date Brian?"

Shari looked over at Brian, then shook her head. "No. I want to get married. I love him."

In love against the wishes of her family. Apparently, he and Mia had been in the same position, and Mia had given up a Yale education to be with him. Was it smart? He had to admit that it wasn't, but apparently, it had been worth it to his wife. Maybe she hadn't wanted that Yale education. Maybe she'd wanted a ranch life like he did. He had to wonder if she'd ever questioned her choices when he'd been working every spare minute.

"You could get married, you know," Olivia said. "Brian's twenty-three. How old are you?"

"Twenty-one," said.

"If you want to get married, you can," Olivia said. "Legally speaking. No one can stop you. You're both adults."

"We've been talking about a little church wedding," Shari said, and a smile came her lips for the first time. "Nothing huge—just friends and family... A summer wedding with some outdoor catering, and maybe an Empire waist gown with a full skirt. It would hide things so that we could get some really nice pictures. I know a photographer who would give us a pretty good deal."

"And your parents would pay for this?" Olivia asked.

Shari's smile slipped. "If I gave them a bit of time to get used to it. Maybe you could talk to them for us."

"I don't think the wedding details are what's bothering them," Olivia said quietly.

"I know." Shari sighed. "I just always dreamed of a pretty outdoor wedding. And

I've met the guy I love and want to spend my life with. What's so wrong with having a beautiful wedding to celebrate that?"

"They take time, for one," Olivia said. "And we don't have much of that right now."

They'd also take money, and Shari's parents didn't sound like they were anywhere close to throwing much of that around in celebration of their daughter's choices. Sawyer noticed how Brian's fingers moved toward Shari's on the tabletop. They leaned toward each other ever so subtly. The timing might be garbage, but these two loved each other.

"How will you support her?" Sawyer asked Brian.

"I'm a mechanic. I'll keep working."

"What's your health insurance like?" Sawyer pressed. Because that mattered—especially with a pregnant wife.

"It's okay. Not as good as her dad's, and she can stay on his insurance until she's twenty-six." Brian looked up, slightly embarrassed. "But they're thinking longer term—and I guess they don't have a lot of faith in me."

It looked like Brian was up against the same problem Sawyer had had—stuck between her parents' expectations and what he could actually provide himself.

"We might get in a little bit of debt when the baby comes, and if we add a wedding on top of that... But it won't be the end of the world," Shari said with a shake of her head. "Brian's working, and I've got a part-time job at the bank, so with the both of us saving and with my dad's health insurance, what's a bit of debt? We'd have the rest of our lives to pay it off." The table fell silent, and Shari eyed them uncertainly. "We'll be fine."

"Does she know?" Olivia asked her brother quietly.

Sawyer frowned slightly. What was the big secret here?

Brian sighed and scraped his fingers through his already mussed hair, then he cast her an apologetic look. "Shari, my sister and I owe two hundred thousand dollars—give or take—in medical fees for our mother's cancer treatment."

Sawyer blinked in surprise—this was the first time he was hearing about this, too. Olivia was in serious debt? He hadn't known…was that something he'd remember later on, or had she never told him? Olivia glanced over at Sawyer and her cheeks pinked slightly—embarrassment? Yeah, he understood that feeling of not wanting your vulnerabilities made public.

"You owe…" Shari seemed to be doing a bit of mental math, because her face paled even more. "How are you going to pay that off, Brian? That's like a mortgage!"

"We have a repayment plan," he said woodenly.

"How long will it take?" she asked.

"With the interest working against us, and both my sister and I paying into it, about twenty years," he said woodenly.

"And we're having a baby!" Her voice was starting to rise. "How are we supposed to do this? I wanted to take some time off work…but even if I went back straight after the baby's born, we'd still have to pay for day care! And diapers. And formula. And… and…" Tears welled in her eyes. "And the wedding… Why didn't you tell me this?"

"Because we'd only started dating!" Brian retorted. "You don't lay out all your financial stuff right away."

"But we're talking about getting married here!" she exclaimed.

Brian fell silent, and he pulled his hand away from Shari's, leaning back in his seat.

"Does the wedding matter so very much?" Olivia asked softly. "I mean a big wedding. You could do something small and very cheap and be just as married."

"It isn't just the wedding now, is it? I don't want to be a single mother, but I don't want to be poor, either!" Shari shook her head. "How will we raise our child? How will be buy a house? I'm going to need a car, too, you know."

From what Sawyer could tell, Shari had a few expectations, too. This wasn't just about her parents wanting more for her.

"Hey…" Sawyer said, keeping his voice

low. "So there have been a few surprises, but that's how life goes. You two are about to be parents, and that's terrifying. I get it. I'm a dad, too, and it scares me every day. But it's also the best thing you'll ever do. My wife died, and I'm pretty sure that wasn't part of my plan for raising my kids, either. But you do what you have to do, and it's worth it. A wedding is just one day…"

"It's more than a day, it's a woman's rite of passage!" Shari retorted. She was getting angry now, from what Sawyer could tell.

"I got kicked in the head by a cow," Sawyer said bluntly, and Shari blinked at him. "My memory is still coming back, but I remembered my daughters' birth. I still don't remember my wedding. A wedding is nice. Don't get me wrong. But it's just one day."

Shari sucked in a shaky breath.

"Vows last," he added. "A marriage matters. If you love him, don't let dreams of a dress and catering hold you back, because that's the kind of regret that will last longer that wedding photos."

Olivia shot Sawyer a grateful look, and she reached over and squeezed his hand under the table. It was a quick movement, and she pulled away just as fast, but the warmth of her fingers over his had felt nice. She wanted to fix this—he could tell. And for her sake, he sure hoped these two would patch it up, grow up, and make a life together. But some things couldn't be forced.

"Now, Shari, what do you want?" Sawyer softened his tone.

Shari turned her tear-filled gaze toward Brian, and she shrugged weakly. "I need to talk to my parents. I can't just break their hearts and push them away."

Brian nodded. "Yeah, you should do that."

"I'm going to call my dad," Shari said, sliding out of the booth and standing up. "He'll give me a ride, and I'll call you soon, okay? I just need...a bit of time."

"What do you mean, he'll give you a ride?" Brian asked, standing up, too.

"I want to go home for a bit. Talk to them."

Her lips trembled. "My dad will come pick me up and I can hash this out with them."

"I should come—" Brian took a step forward.

"No." Shari shook her head. "You shouldn't. I need to talk to them alone."

Shari leaned into his arms, and they clung to each other for a moment, murmured a few things. Then she pulled away, leaving Brian standing there looking empty and frustrated. Shari pulled out her phone and headed for the door, glancing back once with tears in her eyes.

Was this the end for them? Sawyer couldn't tell, but there was an ache in his chest, and this all felt rather familiar somehow.

"For what it's worth, man," Sawyer said, "you can't just cut her family out. I tried that, apparently, and while I don't remember much of it, they don't just go away. She's got a family, and you're going to have to deal with them."

"Yeah? Well, I'm not enough for them,"

Brian said curtly. "And they figure I can't provide for her."

"Prove them wrong," Sawyer retorted. "Find a way. You've got a child to take care of now."

"I don't think I can."

Young. That was all Sawyer could think, looking at Brian. He didn't blame him for not being ready for this. The order was all wrong. Marriage was supposed to come first, then kids. But regardless of the order of events, Brian wasn't going to be able to just brush her family aside. Shari obviously loved them deeply, and they were protective of their daughter, even if that was manifesting itself a little intensely right now.

All normal, as far as Sawyer could see. He had two daughters he was protective of, too.

"I'm going to head out," Brian said hollowly. "Thanks for trying, Olivia."

"I'm sorry," she said. "She had to know about the debt, though."

"I know," he said. "I should have told her

sooner. Never seemed like the right time to bring it up, though."

"You've got a baby coming. There are a lot of things you'll have to talk through that might have waited a bit longer otherwise," Olivia said. "I'm sure you'll work it out."

"I hope so. Thanks anyway."

Brian headed toward the door, his shoulders slumped. Shari was standing where they could see her out the window, and Brian joined her. They both crossed their arms, and didn't touch each other. Olivia rubbed her hands over her face, then looked over at Sawyer.

"Life is never simple, is it?" she asked softly.

Her eyes looked tired and sad, but his gaze kept tugging down to her pink lips. No, it wasn't. Because right now, all he wanted was to kiss her and for just a moment take all that pressure off of her shoulders.

But that wouldn't be right, either. He had to keep his focus here—he had a lot to make up to his daughters, and getting entangled in a romance wasn't going to let him put his focus where it belonged. Besides, she'd made it clear that she wasn't going to be sticking around, and he respected her reasons. He had to stop this. They'd agreed that friendship was where they needed to stop—and they'd been right about that.

"No, it doesn't seem to be." He reached forward and touched her cheek with the back of his finger—the one brief contact he'd allow himself. "It'll be okay."

"You sure?" she asked.

"Eventually," he said, dropping his hand. "One way or another..."

And he meant that about more than just her brother's situation. He meant about his own, too. Now that he knew where he'd gone wrong in the past, he could fix it. And he wouldn't mess it up this time around.

Olivia's mind was spinning as they got back into the truck. Her brother had asked her for help, and she wasn't sure she'd provided any. If anything, she and Sawyer had been a sounding board while Brian and Shari had gotten increasingly overwhelmed. Just once for Brian, after all he'd been through, could love be enough?

Sawyer hopped into the driver's seat and Olivia put her seat belt on. The day was sunny and bright, and despite her brother's troubles, something in the air had the feeling of hope. She'd been praying in her heart for God to work through this situation, and she still believed He would. Unfortunately, Brian and Shari would have to rely on God, if they were willing to try, because as much as Olivia wanted to help, she'd done all she could.

Sawyer pulled out his cell phone and typed in a text.

"What are you doing?" Olivia asked.

"Checking up on the girls," he said. "Seeing if Lloyd's okay with them."

Being a dad, in other words. She put on her seat belt and leaned back. This wasn't the old Sawyer anymore—he was different, deeper, older. Even without his memory, she could see how he'd changed.

"Lloyd says everything's fine," Sawyer said, dropping his phone into his lap and reaching for his seat belt. "He says to take our time. You want to go back, or should we just drive for a bit?"

Olivia smiled gratefully. "Let's just drive."

Sawyer put the truck into Reverse. "That sounds good to me, too."

"So, what's happening with this Evelyn woman?" Olivia asked.

Sawyer backed out of the spot and headed for the road. "I don't know. He likes her—that's clear. But… I'm not sure. She's gorgeous and young, and he's—" Sawyer winced, not finishing the statement.

"He's…a more unique guy," she said.

"Yeah." He cast her a look. She knew what he meant. Lloyd was awkward, in both appearance and personality, but endearingly so. "I don't know. I'm kind of afraid that he's going to get his heart broken here."

"You can't exactly stop that from happening," she replied. "No more than I can fix Brian's situation."

"I understand," he said.

"Do you have any idea what she wants from him?" Olivia asked.

"To see cattle?" Sawyer shook his head. "I don't know! She could have her pick of guys, but she lands on my bachelor uncle. I actually doubt that she's out to bleed him dry or anything. I kind of worry she's just being friendly, and he's getting his hopes up for something more."

"He's a grown man, though," she said. "He can take care of himself."

"I know. Not like I can do anything about it, anyway."

They drove to an intersection, and Sawyer signaled a left-hand turn.

"Do you know where you're going?" she asked.

"Nope. I figure with you here, I can't get too lost."

Olivia laughed at that. He was probably right. She knew this area just as well as anyone else, having grown up here. Sawyer took another left and headed for a straight stretch of road.

"I don't know if I'll ruin it by saying it out loud," Sawyer said quietly. "But this is familiar."

"You're remembering more, aren't you?" she asked.

"Yeah. This and that. It doesn't always connect, but I'm getting more back."

He eased onto the gravel road and stepped on the gas. It felt good to be driving with him—not quite like old times, either. They'd both changed over the years, and this new connection they had was different than in the past. Maybe maturity had made whatever kept tugging them back together sweeter.

"Did I know about the hospital debt?" Sawyer asked.

"No," she said quietly.

"There was a lot I didn't know about you, wasn't there?" He cast her a searching look, and she saw sadness in his gaze.

"I wasn't one to air my problems," she said,

then sighed. "Besides, when my mother died and the hospital sent us the bills, you had Mia. You weren't mine to lean on at that point."

Or to confide in. Those were lines she couldn't cross with a married man, or a nearly married man, no matter how close they used to be.

"Yeah... I get it." He looked over at her again. "So, are you okay now?"

"Me?" she said, surprised. "I'm fine."

"Are you sure?" he asked. "Because I didn't know you guys were under that kind of stress."

"Yes. But it's sweet of you to ask."

Sawyer slowed at a side road, then turned once more. "Where does this lead?"

"The lake," she said.

He nodded. "That sounds good. Did we ever come here together?"

"No," she said. "But this is where my brother and I scattered my mom's ashes."

"Yeah?" he asked. "Should we turn back?"

"No, it'll be nice to come out here again. It's cheerier this time of year. Happier."

Sawyer took the turn, and the narrow road bumped them along, some twigs scraping the passenger side windows. This drive didn't lead to the main beach where all the amenities were, but it had the kind of beach access that young people discovered and then kept secret. The road erupted into a clearing just before the rocky shore of the lake. There were some tire tracks from other vehicles that had parked out here.

Sawyer stopped the truck, and for a moment, they just sat there in the quiet.

"I used it all up," Olivia said after a moment. "Brian was right about that. I took all my mother's savings and everything she could borrow and got my degree. I wasn't even thinking about Brian. I figured she'd save more, and I'd pitch in, and he'd be fine. But look at him now…"

"That isn't your fault," Sawyer said quietly.

"It might not have been intentional, but it's very much my fault," she replied. "Shari's used to better things than our family can offer her. And Brian loves her…but all he can show is a pile of debt he has no hope of crawling out from under. And that isn't either of our faults, but I know how much he wants to build his own business. I got my dreams—my education, my career… Sure, he can work for someone else, but he wants his own shop. And as things stand, he can't do that."

Sawyer was silent, but he reached over and took her hand in his. His palm was warm, and his fingers closed around hers.

"We shouldn't…" she murmured.

"I don't care," he said, his voice low and gravelly. "Sometimes you need someone to hold your hand. You can't do it all alone, Olivia."

"I think I've done all I can, really," she admitted. "Besides working some overtime and sending Brian a bit of cash to help them get ready for the baby."

"You mean here in Beaut," he said, turned toward her. "You've done all you can here."

"Yes." She swallowed against a lump in her throat. "Your memory is coming back nicely, and my brother will sort out his own relationship. Besides, I have to go back to work."

She'd come out here to reconcile Sawyer to the Whites, but she couldn't see a way to do that anymore, either. He'd talk to them, or he wouldn't. She couldn't stick herself in the middle. This morning, she'd said her piece on that subject, and he'd said his. And whatever she'd hoped when she arrived, her contribution wasn't going to warrant the Whites intervening with the hospital board. She'd been naive to even go along with that plan.

"I think I must have missed you," Sawyer said quietly. "The last few years."

"Why do you think that?" she asked with a soft laugh. "You don't remember."

"Because I've known you again for a week, and the thought of you leaving makes my chest heavy," he said, and he lifted her hand to his lips and kissed her fingers.

The gesture was so gentle and sweet that

it brought tears to her eyes. "I missed you so much—"

But she shouldn't even be saying that. She clamped her mouth shut.

"If you stuck around, we could do more of this," he said with a small smile. "We could hang out. We could take the girls to the park. I could take you riding. It would be nice."

"It would." She dropped her gaze. Very nice—while she was secluded away from the rest of the town, at least. But life wasn't lived closeted away from the world. People came with families and communities. It couldn't be sidestepped, and Beaut couldn't be hers.

"But you can't stay," he said.

"No. My life is in Billings now, away from bad memories and nasty rumors. I have a good job, I'm ever so slowly paying off that debt—" She raised her gaze to meet his. "Besides, you keep forgetting that I drive you crazy."

"Yeah, I keep forgetting that." His dark gaze met hers and he smiled, showing he wasn't completely serious. Maybe he needed to be driven nuts every once in a while. What did she know?

Sawyer reached over and moved a curl away from her eyes. The movement was tender, familiar, and afterwards, he didn't move his hand away from her face. His gaze met hers, and he leaned forward. She should pull back—she knew it—but she couldn't bring herself to. Instead, she tipped her face into his palm.

His lips touched hers delicately at first, and when she leaned into him, his kiss became more confident. He released her hand and pushed his fingers into her hair and behind her neck. Everything else seemed to vanish around her, all but his mouth on hers and the feeling of those strong fingers tugging her closer. His lips were warm and soft, and when he pulled back, she found herself breathless. His face was still close to hers, and she could feel the tickle of his breath against her lips.

She closed her eyes, wishing they could do that again. She just wanted to lay her head against his shoulder, feel the beating of his heart… He was like coming home—if home could exist in a bubble away from everyone else.

"Um… I didn't mean to do that…" he breathed.

"I know," she whispered. "And we can't do that anymore."

He licked his lips, then released her, the space between them suddenly feeling like a gulf.

"Have we done that before?" he asked.

"No…" She leaned her head back and shut her eyes. And there was good reason for that. Kisses like this one had a way of prying their way into hearts, making people hope for impossible things.

"So that was a first?" Sawyer asked.

She turned her head to look at him and found his gentle gaze enveloping her.

"That was," she said. "And a last."

"Just checking." He let out a long breath. "I know we'd said we wouldn't go there, but if we have to say goodbye, I'd rather do it without regrets, and I'd regret not kissing you."

"We've been through this before," she said. "Because if we start something—"

"I know."

He belonged with his family—he always had. Longing clamped down on Olivia's throat. They were playing with fire, and they were no longer young enough to think they could come out unsinged.

"I'm sorry..." Sawyer started the truck. "We should probably get back."

He put both hands on the steering wheel, and he swallowed hard.

"We should go," she agreed.

Real life couldn't be avoided forever. He had daughters waiting for him, and she had to get back to her life in Billings before she made it even more complicated to leave.

Whatever attraction it was that kept tugging them together wasn't enough to undo the crushing opinion of the town at large. The rumors, the nastiness, the overt bullying—it had chipped away at her sense of self-worth, and she couldn't allow herself to be pushed back down underneath it again. She couldn't go back to bracing herself every time she went to the store, or forcing a polite smile when she wanted to retaliate against a subtle dig. She couldn't be that woman again—the one who felt like she had to defend herself at every turn.

Not even for Sawyer.

Chapter Twelve

Sawyer headed back down the road the way they'd come, his heart still beating just a bit faster than normal. Because he couldn't remember any other kisses. For him, right now, this was the first kiss in his memory, and whatever instincts he'd had had taken over…

But he shouldn't have done it. He'd been trying to get his footing, but one thing he knew for certain was that he had to make smart choices about what was best, not just for him but for his children. He might regret not kissing Olivia just once, but he'd regret messing up with his daughters a whole lot more. His focus needed to be on them, not on romance. They were still little—he could fix this if he focused and worked hard enough. This was a fresh start for him, and maybe he didn't need Olivia's reassurance that he was a good man. He needed to work his tail off and prove it.

"Turn left up here," Olivia said softly, and he slowed for the turn. These roads were starting to feel more familiar now, a combination of driving them recently and his returning memories.

Sawyer glanced over at Olivia. Her cheeks were still pink, and he couldn't help but notice how beautiful she was. He wanted to reach over and hold her hand, but he wouldn't. He was the one taking this too far—it wasn't her fault.

The next couple of turns, Sawyer remembered without prompting. Things were getting easier, and he could tell that he'd be back to some semblance of normal pretty soon. His roots were sinking deep again with every memory that came back and every new one that he made with his daughters and his uncle on this land. Except Olivia had been a part of that, too, and when she left, she'd leave an aching hole behind.

The West Ranch was coming up, and he signaled the turn. He was home. He could feel it in his gut—that sensation of everything settling down into a comfortable rhythm like a heartbeat. He turned into the drive and followed it around. As he approached the house, he saw two extra vehicles parked next to his uncle's truck, a shiny black sedan and a large wine-colored SUV that looked expensive to both drive and buy. One would be Evelyn's...

"I wonder who's here," Sawyer said.

He glanced over at Olivia, and saw that the blood had drained from her face. He looked back toward the vehicles, anxiety ramping up inside of him.

"What's wrong?" he asked.

"I know that SUV." She let out a shaky breath. "I'm so sorry, Sawyer. I had no idea they'd just show up like this—"

"Who?" But as his stomach sank, he already knew the answer.

Olivia met his gaze with a pleading one of her own. "Mia's parents."

Sawyer's brain spun, and he looked at that SUV once more as he parked. Mia's parents, who'd been so furious that their daughter had lowered herself to his level that they'd cut her off. His girls' grandparents, who now said they wanted to make up, get to know him, get access to his daughters.

He parked the truck behind his uncle's and hopped out. He had a bad feeling about this.

Lord, guide me, he prayed silently.

Olivia slammed her door shut and followed him a couple of steps behind as he headed for the front door. He wasn't really keen on meeting these people, but he also didn't want to leave his daughters around them, either, without him there. He pushed open the door and when he stepped inside, the rumble of conversation stopped and all eyes turned to him.

An older man sat with Bella on his knee.

He was slim and wore dress pants and a vest with a starched white shirt. His hair was silver, and his eyes were steel blue. He must be Wyatt White. Next to him was an older woman with hair dyed brown. She wore some expensive-looking wrap around her shoulders that perfectly matched her lipstick. She must be Irene. She looked like an older version of Mia, he realized in a flash. Lloyd stood by the sink, a crying Lizzie in his arms, Evelyn standing next to him looking uncomfortable.

"Hi, there," Sawyer said, breaking the silence. He stepped up to the older man and scooped his daughter out of his arms. That felt better. Lizzie saw him and stopped crying immediately.

"Daddy!" she said plaintively.

"Hi, Lizzie," he said, and he gave her a smile, just for her. Then he turned to look at the interlopers sitting at the table. They shifted in their chairs and smiled at him—a prim kind of smile that hid any real emotion.

"Sawyer," Wyatt said, rising to his feet. "It's been a long time."

Wyatt put his hand out to shake, and Sawyer did the polite thing and shook his hand. He didn't like this, though. It felt off. He glanced back at Olivia behind him, and her face stayed pale.

"Hello, Olivia, dear," Irene said with a smile.

"Hi," Olivia said weakly. "What are you doing here?"

"We were tired of waiting," Wyatt said with a shrug. "We decided to come on down to Beaut ourselves. Sawyer, we heard about your injury. How are you doing now?"

"I'm fine," he said. "Thanks. What can I do for you?"

"We were hoping to talk," Wyatt said, taking his seat again. "We let things get out of hand before, and we want to fix it. I think we've left this gap between us for far too long."

Lloyd cleared his throat, and he and Evelyn exchanged a look.

"We're going to let you all talk," Lloyd said as he eased Lizzie into Olivia's arms. "Nice to see you again, Senator, Mrs. White."

"You, too, Lloyd," Irene said with a smile. "Thank you for the visit. And nice to meet you, Evelyn."

Lloyd took Evelyn's hand and tugged her after him out into the living room. Apparently, Lloyd figured Sawyer would need some privacy for this, and maybe he did. But having Olivia here with him mattered, too. She knew these people, and he didn't even remember them. But there was something about having them in his kitchen that felt like a threat.

"I realize that we've put you on guard by showing up like this," Wyatt said. "In Olivia's defense, she told us that you weren't ready to see us yet, but it's been almost two years since the funeral, and this is ridiculous."

"What is ridiculous, exactly?" Sawyer asked. "From what I understand, you wanted nothing to do with us."

"We were angry," Irene cut in. "We've had some time to think things through. We shouldn't have reacted the way we did. And we're sorry."

Sawyer sighed. Maybe it was time to talk a few things out. He looked over at Olivia, and she gazed back at him, but her expression was guarded. Whose side was she on?

"Tell us about the girls," Irene added when he hadn't answered her. "What sorts of things do they like? What kind of toys—"

"I don't need gifts," Sawyer interrupted. "I need to understand what happened."

Sawyer pulled out a chair for Olivia, and one for himself, then sat down. Olivia didn't look at the Whites. Instead she stroked a gentle hand over Lizzie's head as the toddler leaned in to be cuddled. Her eyes were drooping.

"The girls are tired," Sawyer said. "It's past their nap time."

"I'll go get them settled," Olivia offered. "If you want. You can keep talking."

Sawyer nodded. It would help. Olivia took

Bella in her other arm and headed out the same direction that Lloyd and Evelyn had gone. Sawyer noticed that Irene's gaze followed the girls as they left the room until Wyatt nudged her and she focused back on Sawyer.

"What do you want to know?" Wyatt asked.

"Why did you hate me so much?" he suggested. That was a good start.

"It wasn't you," Wyatt replied. "It was…we wanted more for our daughter, and it seemed to us that her desire to marry you was rooted in a rebellious phase, not in something worthy of the vows of marriage."

That was insulting. What was he, a drummer with a garage band?

"We were adults," Sawyer countered.

"Yes, yes, and we're admitting that we were wrong," Irene said. "Mia loved you. And we were too stubborn to accept it. But there are children now, and we feel it's important to do what's best for them."

"And what do you think is best for them?" he asked.

"Us," Wyatt said simply, and Sawyer's heart thudded to a stop.

"A relationship with us," Irene amended. "We have a lot to offer our granddaughters. We can get them the best of everything— music lessons, tutors, educational toys… This is what grandparents are *for.*"

"Didn't Olivia tell you this?" Wyatt asked with a frown.

"She brought it up," Sawyer confirmed. "She said you were family and you wanted to make up."

"Well, this is us attempting to reconcile," Wyatt said. "We can do what you can't, Sawyer. We can set them up with the top pediatricians Billings has to offer—"

"Billings?" Sawyer said. "That's a long way off."

"It's where you find the best of everything in this state," Wyatt said. "It's where the specialist doctors are, the most elite preschool programs—"

"I live in Beaut," Sawyer said.

"Yes, but..." Wyatt sighed. "This isn't the time."

"For what?" Sawyer snapped. "What were you hoping for?"

"You are a very busy man," Irene said quietly. "You work so hard, and it can't be easy to be raising two children alone. We're only offering our help. We could be there when you can't. We could hire the most qualified nannies, enroll them in an excellent preschool that sets children up for the brightest futures."

"Mia didn't have that," Sawyer said, and realized as the words came out, that it was true. Mia had been in Beaut...she'd gone to school with Olivia.

"She did at the start. We only moved here when she was in junior high. We thought it was best to mingle..." Irene winced. "For Wyatt's career at the time. But Wyatt's a senator now, and if Mia were alive—"

"No!" Sawyer said, his voice thundering louder than he'd intended. "Don't you do that. You can't tell me what Mia would have wanted!"

He took a deep breath, steadying himself. He wasn't here to bellow at them, but he wouldn't have them manipulating him, either.

"Then think about yourself," Wyatt cut in. "You're single now. Young. Working hard. And you're trying to build a life with two toddlers who need more than you'll ever be able to provide. You don't have to do this alone! We're family."

"And what exactly are you suggesting?" Sawyer asked. Because he could feel it there between the lines—something they didn't quite want to articulate.

Irene licked her lips. "That we provide for the girls, and you would visit just as often as you wanted. Our door would always be open to you. We promise you that. This was why Olivia came out here. She was supposed to talk to you for us, explain our position."

At that moment, Olivia appeared in the doorway, and her gaze met his. Had she brought these people out to see him? Did she really think he'd hand his kids over to these people and let them just take over?

"That's why—" Sawyer started, but the words stuck in his throat. He stared at Olivia. "Is she telling the truth?"

"You didn't say you wanted to take the girls away from him!" Olivia said, her angry gaze sweeping over Irene. "You said you wanted to reconcile, be a part of their lives…"

"That would be the start of it," Wyatt said. "But the more we thought about it, the more we realized that we have to do better by our granddaughters than that."

"No," Sawyer said, his hands balling into fists at his sides. "That's my answer. No! I'm not interested in giving my children up!"

"Do you remember how hard it's been?" Irene asked softly. "Sawyer—do you honestly *remember*?"

He didn't, but something else had come together in his head—a memory forced into the forefront by his pounding adrenaline. Standing at Mia's funeral with his heart breaking—and Wyatt giving him the same offer...

"You suggested this before," Sawyer said slowly. "At Mia's funeral. You said you should raise the girls and let me remarry and move on."

The Whites were silent, watching him nervously. Irene started to fiddle with a bracelet on her wrist and Wyatt's lips started to twitch.

"That's why we haven't spoken in two years," Sawyer went on as the memory finally settled into place in his head. "I'm not some selfish jerk who couldn't forgive a slight from parents who wanted a better match for their daughter. I'm a dad who won't give up his little girls! What makes you think I'd be interested now?" He shook his head slowly. "The answer is still no. No! I will not give up my children! No, I will not send them to live with you so I can pretend I have no other obligations!" His voice was rising and he couldn't help it this time. "I might not remember everything, but I remember my girls! They're mine, and they're my reason for everything I do... It might not be easy, but since when are the good things easy? I'm their father, and I'll provide everything they need—that's a guarantee!" He marched over to the front door and hauled it open. "Now, get out!"

Olivia stared at the Whites in shock. They wanted her to help them convince an injured man to give up his children? She could hardly believe it. Lloyd and Evelyn had come to the doorway between the living room and the kitchen, and for a heart-stopping moment, everything was silence.

"Olivia?" Irene said tightly.

"What?" she demanded. "You told me that you wanted to reconcile! This—whatever this is—is not reconciliation!"

"Things have gotten out of hand here," Wyatt said firmly.

"I'll say!" Olivia shot back. "You asked me to help you to be a family again! How could you think this is what a family looks like? Those girls need their father!"

"We said he could visit!" Irene said testily. "And I'll have you know, young lady, you'd better start holding up your end of the bargain if you expect us to speak on your behalf—"

"I don't expect you to," Olivia shot back. "Keep your influence. I was naive to think you actually wanted to help me to begin with."

Sawyer looked at her questioningly, but she couldn't explain now. The Whites picked up their things and moved toward the door.

"Sawyer, man to man, here—" Wyatt began.

"Man to man, you'd better leave before I get really angry," Sawyer snapped back, and Wyatt took his wife's hand and they swept out the door. Sawyer swung it shut with a bang that made Olivia's heart jump in her chest.

"What's happening?" Lloyd asked.

Sawyer rubbed a hand over his face. "I'm

not really sure. But I have a feeling that Mia's parents had bigger plans for my daughters than anyone else realized."

Olivia felt tears rise in her eyes. "I had no idea, Sawyer. I promise you that. I would never have spoken for them if I'd realized what they wanted!"

"Yeah..." He heaved a sigh, then he looked toward the hallway. "Did we wake the girls up?"

Evelyn slipped away to check—she and Lloyd had been caring for the girls all morning, after all—and Lloyd went to the window.

"They've just pulled out," Lloyd said, his voice low. "Do you think that's the last of them?"

"No idea..." Sawyer looked deflated now, tired, and Olivia slid her hand into his.

"They're sleeping still," Evelyn said, coming back into the room. "But listen, if you need any help at all, Sawyer—"

"No, I'm fine for now," Sawyer said, and he tightened his grip on Olivia's hand.

"Why don't I take you out to the barn," Lloyd said, looking over at Evelyn. "We can give these two some space. I think the worst is over."

Evelyn nodded and while they got their coats and headed outside, Olivia looked up into Sawyer's face.

"I'm sorry," she whispered.

What else could she say? She felt horrible that she'd been part of this at all, but she hadn't known that the Whites wanted to take their granddaughters away from him! Her mind was still spinning, trying to catch up. Was this what the Whites had become?

"I'm really sorry." Tears misted her eyes.

"I know." Sawyer rubbed his hands over his face.

"I had no idea..."

"What were they talking about, speaking on your behalf?"

Olivia swallowed back the lump in her throat. "They said they'd speak to the hospital board to help lower our debt if I helped them to reconcile with you. I didn't tell you

about it right away, because you couldn't remember, and then when I brought it up, you
knew where you stood already—you said
you'd talk to them when you were ready. And
that was fair. I knew then that I wouldn't get
the favor from them, so there didn't seem to
be any point in bringing it up."

He was silent for a moment, then nodded
slowly. "And you were willing to walk away
from that kind of help?"

"Yes. I wasn't going to take advantage of
you, Sawyer. I couldn't do that! You don't
remember what we were to each other, but
I've always—" She stopped, biting back the
words. She was saying too much.

"You've always what?" His dark eyes met
hers, and she couldn't hold the words back
anymore. She'd been trying to protect him
while he recovered, but hiding all those motives and feelings hurt too much. It was time
he knew it all.

"I've always loved you. When I shouldn't.
When you weren't mine to love. When you
didn't love me back. I loved you," she said,

her voice trembling. "You told me you needed space with Mia because you loved her, and I gave it to you because I was trying to cut off the last of my feelings for you. I thought I had... And I'm only telling you now because I can't have you believe that I'd do anything to hurt you or to separate you from your children."

"You *thought* you had cut off your feelings for me," he said. "But?"

Olivia had already said too much, and felt a wave of panic.

"Olivia—" His voice was deep and firm. He caught her hand and tugged her closer. "Did you succeed in that? Did you stop loving me?"

She didn't answer, but tears filled her eyes. How could she? Just looking up at him right now, her heart wanted to tear in two.

"Because I love you," he breathed. "I knew it when I saw you again—and it was more than you just being a comfort in a difficult time. I don't remember everything yet, but I know what you mean to me now..."

Sawyer's lips came down over hers. She dug her fingers into the sides of his shirt and leaned into him as his lips moved over hers. His kiss was filled with longing and when he pulled back, she blinked blearily up at him.

"I love you, too," she said, but then she took another step away from him, lest he kiss her again. She couldn't think straight in his arms—it felt too warm and sweet there.

"But?" he asked huskily.

"I'm not staying here, Sawyer," she said, shaking her head. "I've worked too hard to push my life forward! Besides, I can't make enough here. I barely make enough in Billings, what with the money that's taken off my paycheck to pay back the hospital. My life isn't exactly fixed, yet... Besides, what if I did stay?"

"I'd be real happy," Sawyer said. "What do you think?"

"What would we be to each other?" she asked. "Friends who keep falling into each other's arms? Is this even healthy?"

Sawyer stilled. "I'm trying to be a better

dad than I was before, and I need to put the hard work in—"

"I know," she said. "You need to focus on your kids. So you want me to stay and be here for you without needing more. But we can't sit here in this purgatory of friendship where we can't be what our hearts want us to be. We've done that before. It was awful. Even if I could afford to stay in Beaut, even if I could make a life here in this town that tore away my self-esteem…you're starting over, too. You have to be the dad your girls need. So if I stayed, then what? I can't just be your buddy, pretending I don't feel this! And you can't do that either. We can't do this to ourselves."

"We've done this before," he said sadly. "I just don't remember it yet."

"You will," she whispered. "It hurt us both."

He nodded.

"We set up our rules for good reason," she said. "Before it was because I wasn't staying, and we wanted to avoid this exact problem..."

From the bedroom, the sound of a toddler's cry filtered out toward them, a plaintive, lonely wail.

Olivia licked her lips. "Go take care of your girls, Sawyer."

"Are you leaving?" he asked.

"Yes." She nodded, her chin trembling. "I'll get my bag."

"Will I see you before you leave town?" he asked.

The toddler's cry turned into two, and he looked at her with heartbreak in his deep brown eyes. He was torn—she could feel it. His girls needed his help, and she couldn't stay in limbo with him anymore.

"I don't know," she admitted. "But your girls need you."

Sawyer moved toward the hallway this time, and when he looked back over his shoulder, she had to hold herself back from running into his arms. She'd get her bag and go find a hotel room for the night. She couldn't leave town without talking to Brian once more, but she couldn't wrap up her own business from here—not where her heart kept trying to settle down and make a home.

Olivia had fallen in love with Sawyer all over again... Why couldn't she learn that this man could never be hers?

Chapter Thirteen

Olivia sat beside her bag on the hotel room bed, staring at the empty TV screen. Her heart felt like it would crack in two within her chest, and she put her hand over the spot over her breastbone as tears spilled down her cheeks.

She loved him… That had always been the problem. She'd thought she could put her feelings aside when went to school, but it hadn't worked. She'd left him in her best friend's arms and told herself that he wasn't hers to care for—which had been true. But it didn't make it any easier to cut him out of her heart.

Her life wasn't here anymore, and she couldn't just come back, either. She could make more in Billings to help her brother—and she could be more, and be happier with herself, there. Beaut would always be the place that had run her into the ground. Fresh starts in a town like this weren't even possible with amnesia.

And knowing all of that…knowing that Sawyer couldn't let himself be with her, either, didn't change the fact that her heart was breaking. She lay down on the bed and let the tears flow. This town had broken her once before, and she'd vowed that she'd never let herself be shredded like that again. She'd known better, but somehow she'd still fallen for this man.

As she lay on the bed, her eyes drooped shut, and she fell in to a deep, empty slumber. An hour later, Olivia awoke with a parched throat. Her cell phone beside her was buzzing, and she picked it up, looking at the number. Her brother…

"Hi, Brian," she said.

"Hey…are you okay?" Her brother's voice lowered. "You sound like you've been crying."

"I'm fine," she said, pushing herself up. "I fell asleep."

"Okay…" He didn't sound convinced. "Is everything okay with you and Sawyer?"

"We're friends," she said. "We always will be."

"You seemed like more when I saw you—"

Were her feelings for the man so obvious? She rubbed her hand over her puffy eyes. "We're friends," she repeated. "I don't want to talk about that right now, okay?"

"I just wanted to let you know that I've sorted things out with Shari," he said.

"Have you?" she asked hopefully.

"That pastor dropped by."

"Oh?" She hesitated. "Are you mad?"

"Nah… His timing was good, I guess. We had a long talk. He had a lot to say about you, actually."

"I thought he might…" She winced. "I told

him how much I wanted to make up with you, and..."

"Yeah, he pointed out just how important family is, and that's not just a religion thing. It's a life thing, and it kind of applied to me and Shari, too. Sawyer was right that I can't separate her from her family. And they want to make sure she's okay—that her pregnancy is safe, and all that. They loved her before I did, so..."

"Oh, Brian..." This didn't sound good. Was her family breaking the couple up?

"No, it's okay," he said quickly. "I talked to her father, and they want her to have a proper wedding. Those take time to plan. We aren't ready for a baby, she and I, but I love her. So we're going to slow this down. I'm going to work really hard, save up, and we'll get married after the baby is born."

"Oh!" Olivia smiled through her own sadness. "That's a good idea."

"And her dad is going to hire me at the truck yard that he owns. He needs a good mechanic, and it'll pay better than the job

I've got now. I can show him what I'm made of, earn his respect. I think he needs to see firsthand that I'm the kind of guy who will take care of her."

Her brother was making some mature choices here, and she felt a wave of love for him. At least it could work out for one of them.

"That sounds like a great plan, Brian," she said. "I'm really proud of you."

"And..." He sighed. "You'll like this part—Shari and I agreed to start going to church with her grandma once a month. You know—family ties and all that."

Olivia couldn't help but smile. "Church can't hurt, Brian."

"I beg to differ. Whatever," Brian said, but his tone had softened. "Maybe it won't be so bad. I kind of like the pastor. Besides, her grandmother is getting on in years, and this is a relationship that matters to Shari. So I can be flexible."

"I'm glad," she said. "And I mean it—I'm really proud."

"Thanks. I'm going shopping for a ring this afternoon," he said. "She deserves a proper proposal. I'm not just marrying her because of the baby, and I want her family to know that, too. A ring sends a message."

"I think so, too," Olivia agreed.

"Okay, well, just wanted to let you know. Thanks for being here for me. I know I've been hard on you, but I think it's time I make the life I want, instead of just being mad that you had it easier."

"Not as easy as you think," she said quietly. "I'm still working hard to help pay that debt off. I've been putting some extra on top of my share of the monthly payments, you know. We'll get rid of it, eventually."

"The Whites won't help?" Brian asked.

"I'm afraid not. It's okay. We'll just keep moving forward, right? You've got Shari and the baby now—let's keep those priorities in sight. A dad has to put his kids first."

"Yeah. And I want you to come back next month so Shari's family can meet you. They

want to have a big dinner and you're the clos-
est family I've got. Will you come?"

"Yes, of course," she said. "I'm going back
to Billings in the morning, though. I need to
be in my own apartment again."

"Are you sure you're okay?" Brian asked.

"I'm sure..." She was doing as well as
could be expected under the circumstances.
Olivia was missing Sawyer and the way he
made her feel. She was missing the toddlers,
too. They'd settled right into her heart. Being
in the safest place she knew wasn't going to
be enough. Not this time. "But I'll be back
for the dinner. Give me a call later and tell
me when and where."

"Thanks," Brian said. "I'd better go. I'm
standing in front of the jewelry store, so..."

"Pick something beautiful," she said with
a misty smile.

"Yeah. I will. See you."

After saying goodbye, Olivia hung up the
call and looked down at the phone in her
hand. Brian would be okay...and it sounded
like his new in-laws would help him learn the

next steps. Waiting on that wedding wasn't a terrible idea. Brian and Shari were both young and scared, and some family support never hurt. Mia would have given anything to have had a little bit of that…

God had worked out a reconciliation for her and Brian after all, and it hadn't included any favors from Mia's family. Brian had some new promise in his future and it was all happening right here in Beaut with the girl he'd fallen for. Olivia had failed in her mission for Mia's parents, but her prayers had all been answered.

Olivia would head back to Billings in the morning like she'd said, but before she left, she had one more thing she wanted to do, and that was to visit Mia's grave…alone. She had a few things to say to her best friend…

Olivia left her bag on the bed and grabbed her purse. Today, she'd have that time with her own grief—her memories, her dashed hopes for the future. And then she'd go back to Billings. She'd continue to make that city home, and put one foot in front of the other.

The drive to the little country church took a few minutes, and when she arrived, the sun shone low and golden. She parked her car and when she got out, she pulled her jacket a little closer around herself.

She paused at the gate to the graveyard, and looked down at that familiar verse: "Blessed are they that mourn; for they shall be comforted."

Maybe her comfort would come, too. At long last. But she was mourning more than her friend. She was mourning the man she'd fallen in love with, her own sense of safety and goodness that had been shattered in this town. She'd lost so much in the last few years, and perhaps if she could take the time to cry over a little of it, she could find some healing, too.

Olivia made her way through the gravestones toward her friend's little flat marker, and she sank down to a crouch beside it. Tears ebbed close to the surface, but she sat there, dry-eyed.

"I wanted to come here and cry for you, Mia..." she murmured aloud.

Olivia's heart felt empty and sodden, and as she looked at Mia's grave, all she could think about were all those hopes for the future that they'd both shared. Life had been harder than anticipated...for all of them. But Olivia had faced those challenges. And now, she was no longer the young woman reeling from this town's cruelty. She'd grown up and she'd toughened up.

"It's going to be okay..." she whispered, and she realized she wasn't talking to Mia anymore. This was for herself. It would be okay, eventually. God would bring her that promised comfort.

"Olivia?"

Olivia startled and turned to see Irene standing behind her. She was wearing the same dark pink wrap from earlier, but she looked older this afternoon. Her earlier confidence and easy smiles seemed to be gone, and the lines in her face were deeper.

"Irene..." Olivia swallowed hard and she rose to her feet. "I came to see her grave."

"Me, too," Irene said.

Mia's mother probably needed space at this grave, too, and maybe it was time for Olivia to leave anyway. "I'll give you some privacy."

"No, that's okay," Irene said, and she wound her way through the other gravestones and stopped at Olivia's side. "You should stay."

"I understand needing some time alone with Mia," Olivia said.

"I'm glad you're here," Irene said with a small shake of her head. "I'm embarrassed about earlier."

Irene seemed more like herself out here, more like the woman Olivia had known for years. That poised, manipulative woman from earlier...what had that been?

"Sawyer's a good man, you know," Olivia said softly. "He's a good father."

Irene nodded and her chin trembled.

"He won't give them up, either—" Olivia looked over at Irene, wondering what her plan was after this. Were they going to fight Sawyer for custody now that they knew about his injury?

"They're my little girl's babies," Irene whispered. "And I lost Mia… You don't know what it's like to bury your child. I remember her as a newborn. It's like yesterday that I cradled her in my arms."

Irene wrapped her arms around herself, and Olivia slid an arm around Irene's slim shoulders. For a long moment, the two women stood there looking down at the simple stone that commemorated the life of Mia White West.

"You can still be grandparents," Olivia said. "You can be the ones who bring the girls gifts from the city. You can come visit and see their school recitals. You can invite them to visit you for a week in the summer—if Sawyer would allow that now…"

Irene wiped a tear from her cheek, and her next words came out with venom. "I hate this town."

Olivia looked over at her in surprise. "What?"

"I hate this place," Irene whispered hoarsely. "I hate it so much that it hurts. We came here to start out my husband's political career, and it worked. He hit the ground running, but I had to give up everything to come. I had to sacrifice the life I loved in Billings, the friends, the security... And we even put Mia in a public school so that later on, no one could say that we were too privileged and didn't understand regular people." Her lips turned down in disgust. "And what happened? Mia fell in love with a ranch hand..." Irene squeezed her eyes shut. "I sacrificed so much, and the sacrifices just keep coming. I *hate* this place. I hate that my baby is buried here. I hate that my grandchildren are being raised here... This town took everything from me!"

"I know the feeling," Olivia said, and she licked her lips, trying to control her emotion. "I left and I never meant to come back—"

"Those rumors." Irene nodded. "They were vicious."

"Yeah…" Olivia sucked in a tremulous breath. "I was so young…why did they do that me? Why did anyone believe any of it? I was just a girl who was doing her best to get some good grades and become a nurse. I mean, the boys who told the lies—yeah, I'd embarrassed them. But the rest—what had I done to them?"

Irene shook her head. "People do stupid things when they get caught up in groups." She shrugged. "People do stupid things on their own, too."

"I don't trust the people here any more than you do," Olivia said softly. "But this isn't about the town, Irene. This is about Mia's little girls. And about their dad."

Irene sighed. "I'm not going to try and take them from him, you know."

"I'm glad," she said. "They belong with their father."

"So how does someone start over, then? How do I do that?" The older woman turned toward her, her watery eyes searching Olivia's face for answers. "How is that even possible? Are Wyatt and I supposed to come out here, cap in hand, begging for a chance to even see the girls?"

"Maybe at first." Olivia shrugged weakly.

"I can't do that..." Irene's lips trembled. "No."

"Sawyer is a good man—a deeply good man. He's not interested in making you grovel, but he does need to be able to trust your intentions. And in turn, you have to trust in the basic goodness of people," Olivia said with a helpless shrug. "You'll have to believe that Sawyer can forgive you, that this town can cradle Mia when your arms aren't able... That Sawyer can see how much you loved her..."

"He wouldn't forgive us," Irene said with a shake of her head.

"You don't know him like I do, then," she replied. "He's always been fair and down-to-earth. He says what he means. He's trustworthy. He's—" Her voice caught. He was the best man she'd ever known. But this wasn't about her feelings for Sawyer. "You'll have to forgive Beaut for your sacrifices. For Lizzie's and Bella's sakes. Because they need their father, but Irene, they need grandparents, too. You're a family, whether you like it or not. That was Mia's choice, and now you have to find a way to be one. For Mia and for her little girls."

Irene fell silent, and then she heaved a shuddering sigh. Would she be able to humble herself and embrace this town for all its flaws and limitations?

And yet, Olivia's words were echoing inside her own head. Irene needed to forgive this town if she was to get her heart's desire. She'd have to believe in the goodness of others… Could Olivia do that, too? Could she stand straight and walk back into this town and make a home in it? Could she forgive the people who had crushed her when she was so vulnerable? It was a lot to ask of anyone, and Olivia knew exactly why Irene was holding back. It was *hard*.

"I'm leaving," Olivia said, putting a hand

on Irene's arm. "Let's get together for a coffee in Billings."

Irene nodded, and Olivia turned to leave. But this new thought was brewing inside of her.

Olivia had spent her energy getting out of this town, away from those rumors and the ugly people who spread them… She'd spent her energy rebuilding herself and finding a safe place to grow her life. Those were good things! But what if it were possible to forgive Beaut? What if it were possible to believe in the basic goodness of the people here, and trust them to change, grow, make a space for her?

Could she do that?

Fresh starts were painful and oh, so risky. They involved a lot of bravery, whether those starts were far from home, or back in the town that had hurt her. Could she do it for Sawyer?

But even if she could start over again, come back to Beaut and face the people who had made her most miserable all those years ago, it didn't change what Sawyer needed.

If she truly loved this man, she'd let him focus on his daughters, and she wouldn't get in his way.

Early that evening, Sawyer sat at the kitchen table with his daughters, who were munching on a snack of dry cereal in their high chairs.

"There are two cows that need help—" Lloyd said, slapping his hat against his jeans. Evelyn stood at the door, her jeans muddied and her hair mussed from the wind, but she looked happy enough. "One in the west pasture and one already in the barn. Toby is with the one in the west pasture, but we need to get down to the barn. And I need your help, Sawyer. This one will require some muscle."

"Now?" Sawyer asked, standing up. "So you'll let me actually help, will you?"

"I don't have a choice," Lloyd snapped. "Do as I say, and we'll get this cow through."

"Would you—" Sawyer turned to Evelyn.

"I'll watch the kids," she said quickly. "Go! I'm fine."

Lloyd shot Evelyn a grin. "You're some woman, you know that?"

Evelyn's face tinged pink, but she didn't answer, and Lloyd was already heading for his boots. Sawyer followed suit and they headed out the door for the truck, the screen slamming behind them.

"It's triplets, we think," Lloyd said as he hopped into the driver's side.

Sawyer banged his door shut, and gave a curt nod. "And you kept her in the barn, knowing she'd need help when the time came."

"You're remembering a bit," Lloyd said, putting the truck into gear and pulling out. "Good. We'll need that."

"It's coming back," Sawyer agreed. And so were a few more memories—his daughters as babies when they first started crawling, and that first Christmas when he and Lloyd had wrapped the presents for the girls so carefully, using up way more tape than was probably necessary. He was remembering a lot now, but nothing was quite so stark or clear in his mind as the look on Olivia's face when he walked away.

It had taken all of his strength—of character and of body—to keep him moving. Because he loved her in a bone-deep kind of way, and getting over that love was going to take a long time. A lump was stuck in his throat, and it had been since their goodbye.

"So she's gone, then?" Lloyd asked as they bumped over a pothole on the road down to the barn.

"Yep," he said, his voice tight.

"You sure you want that?" Lloyd asked, looking over at him.

Sawyer's eyes misted. "No, of course not. But it's what's right. And the right thing is seldom the easy thing."

Lloyd didn't answer. He pulled up in front of the barn and turned off the engine. They both got out, and Lloyd grabbed a few supplies from the back of the truck on his way by. Then they went inside, the smell of cattle and dust settling around them.

A very pregnant cow was pacing in her stall—her head down. Her belly was big and round, and there was a ripple of movement from within. Her hooves scraped against the floor as she walked. There were small hooves showing out the back of her, and when a contraction hit, they didn't move any further. A young ranch hand looked over at them in relief as they came in.

"You go on and do your work," Lloyd said to the young man. "We'll take over."

"Thanks."

Sawyer watched as Lloyd put the chains on the back of the cow and felt around to attach them to the hooves. He knew the process here—it wasn't foggy like some of those other memories, either.

"Okay, this is going to take both of us," Lloyd said. "Wait on the contraction—"

For the next two hours, Lloyd and Sawyer worked with the cow's natural rhythms to deliver three small but healthy calves. The mother let all three suckle, which wasn't the norm but was a blessed relief, and Sawyer leaned back against a rail, watching the newborn animals find their own comfort in their mother.

"Are you sure you're okay with Olivia just leaving?" Lloyd asked again as he refilled a bucket of oats for the cow.

"Look," Sawyer said with a sigh. "I might not remember everything, but I know who I need to be, and that's a dad first."

Lloyd chewed the side of his cheek for a moment, then said, "I'm going to say something."

"All right," Sawyer said with a small smile.

"You work too hard."

Sawyer sighed. "Yeah, I know. Mia said it all the time—I'm a workaholic. But I'll do better. The girls will have my attention. I'll be the dad they need."

"No, I mean you work too hard, period," Lloyd said. "You lost your memory, but you have this gut instinct to work. It's a good thing—most times. I couldn't run this place without you for very long. But you've been working at your recovery, working to get your memories back, working to figure out where you went wrong, and vowing that you'll work to fix it."

"What else am I supposed to do?" Sawyer demanded. "I'm doing everything in my power!"

"Yeah," Lloyd nodded. "But what would happen if you stopped working so hard at everything? What would happen if you just followed your heart for once?"

What if he threw it all to the wind and stopped trying? It was tempting—he had to admit that.

"It would lead me straight to Olivia!" Sawyer said. "And that's not what either of us need right now."

"When you went to work those fields, Sawyer, it was your heart that guided you back home every night to your family. That part wasn't work for you. You can trust your heart to steer you straight, you know. If you have to work against your very heart, son, I think it's a losing battle."

"I need to be a good dad," he said. "I need to keep my priorities straight."

"But being a good dad is about more than hard work," Lloyd said. "If it were about putting your back into it, then providing financially would be enough. But it isn't. Kids need a relationship with you. They need time with you. They need...your heart."

"And that's what I'm trying to give them!" he said, his voice trembling. "I'm giving up the woman I love so that they can have my whole heart. I'm doing my best here!"

Why couldn't Lloyd see that? His heart was in the right place—he wanted to make sure he did this properly. He was willing to sacrifice his own loving relationship to get that for his kids.

"What else is holding you back?" Lloyd asked.

"I hardly know who I am, and I'm not at full capacity here," Sawyer said. "I'm still getting back my memories, and I don't even know if I'll get everything back again. So I have to prioritize things. And my daughters have to come first."

"I agree," Lloyd said with a nod. "But does that mean you can't have love, too?"

"For now, yes," Sawyer replied. "But it's not just me. She can't come back here. She had a really rough time in Beaut, and she can't just step back into life here. It's both of us, Lloyd."

The older man nodded slowly, then shrugged. "Okay. Maybe it won't work with Olivia, but in the future maybe you could quit working so hard—at everything. Just… go with your gut." Lloyd picked up a few of his tools, and he headed for the door. "You coming?"

"In a few minutes," Sawyer replied. "I'll walk up. Go on without me."

"All right, then."

The barn door closed, and Sawyer sucked in a deep breath. His throat felt thick with emotion as he stood there, watching the cow lick one of her calves.

Sawyer had messed up in his family life, and he was trying to make up for past mistakes. But maybe it was time to let those mistakes go to the bottom of the sea, and follow his heart again. Maybe Lloyd was right and he needed to let go a little bit, if his relationships were going to turn out differently.

If Olivia could find a way to make a life here, he wouldn't be able to stop himself from committing himself to her for the rest of his life. If she'd have him, he'd do more than love her...he'd marry her.

The realization hit him in the chest like a bag of rocks. He'd marry her! If he followed his heart like Lloyd suggested, it would lead him right down the aisle without a second thought.

He might not be able to trust his memory fully, but even when he didn't know who he was, his heart had steered him true. Olivia might have meant something to him in the past, but now that he'd discovered her again, she meant everything. Olivia *could* be his second chance at love, and his girls' second chance at a mom.

If she could find it in her own heart to come home to Beaut.

But that might be too much to ask.

Chapter Fourteen

Olivia had meant to drive from the grave-yard back to town directly, but when she approached the turn that led to the West Ranch, she found herself signaling. A truck behind her moved into the other lane to pass, and Olivia felt a tremor in her chest as the huge vehicle rumbled by.

She wasn't sure what she wanted to even say to Sawyer—but she longed to see him. Just once more. Maybe her choice would feel clearer if she could talk it through with him, because her heart was tugging her in a direction she'd never imagined she'd want to go.

She took the turn and as she drove the last

mile, her stomach fluttered. If she stayed...
what then? What would her life look like?
Would Sawyer even want her here?

He'd been clear about where he stood and
what he wanted. He was a dad first and fore-
most, and she understood that. But the idea
of walking away from him was so much
harder than she'd thought.

She pulled into the drive, and followed it
around to the house. As she parked next to
Lloyd's truck, the older man hopped out of
the vehicle and gave her a wave.

"Hey, there," Lloyd said, coming around
to her side. "You're back."

"I—" Olivia turned off the car and opened
the door. "I was hoping to talk to Sawyer, if
he's around."

"He's down at the barn," Lloyd said, an-
gling his head in that direction. "You could
catch him there, no doubt."

"Okay, I'll try that." She smiled gratefully.
"Thanks."

Olivia slammed her door shut and headed

toward the long gravel drive. Behind her the side door to the house opened, and she heard Lloyd's tone soften.

"Kids look good on you, Evelyn."

And Evelyn's soft laugh. "I wouldn't mind three or four of my own."

"You don't say…"

The door closed then, and their voices were cut off from her hearing. Olivia glanced back at the house over her shoulder, and she couldn't help but smile at that. Lloyd was falling for Evelyn, and it seemed like Evelyn wasn't exactly running away from the West Ranch, either. Maybe those two would make something of their relationship, after all.

The sun was sinking, red flooding the sky as the golden orb sunk low and oblong against the horizon. The wind was cool, but not cold, as Olivia walked. A little privacy would be nice—if she made an utter fool of herself, at least she wouldn't have an audience for it, aside from some cows.

The barn door opened and Sawyer came

outside. The door thunked shut behind him, the sound surfing that cool breeze. He pushed his hat down, and then raised his head. It was then that he saw her, because he froze.

Olivia raised her hand in a wave. Did he even want to see her? Was she stupid to have come at all? Her steps slowed, and she considered turning back, but it was too late now. Sawyer had started walking toward her, and as he walked, his steps got faster until he was jogging.

So maybe he did want to talk a bit...her eyes misted with tears, and she picked up her pace, too. When Sawyer reached her, he didn't say a thing—he just wound his arms around her waist, pulled off his cowboy hat, and covered her lips with his.

She sank against his broad chest, drinking in the warmth of him as she kissed him back. When he finally pulled away, she blinked up at him.

"Hi," he breathed.

"I've been thinking about something,"

she said softly. "And I wanted to talk to you about it."

"Tell me you're thinking of coming home to Beaut," he said, his voice a low rumble.

"Actually, I am…" She smiled mistily. "I saw Irene at Mia's grave. I know you don't like them much, Sawyer, and I know they've been rude beyond imagining, and they're completely out of line, but they're family. And they're not graceful people, but they're grieving, too, and—"

"What are you trying to say?" he asked uncertainly.

Olivia sucked in a breath and looked around herself at the barn, the road leading up to the house… Could she do this? Could she forgive a town for crushing her spirit?

"I gave Irene some advice about being able to humble herself and come back to the town she can't stand." Olivia grimaced. "Irene lost a lot in Beaut, and she has some hard feelings, but she wants to do what it takes to earn your trust and to be a grandmother to your girls. Anyway, I told her that coming home meant trusting in people's goodness—yours, namely. If she was to be able to earn your trust and be a part of the girls' lives in a balanced way, she was going to have to trust your basic goodness."

"Okay..." he said uncertainly. "So you came back to get me to talk to her?"

"No..." She laughed softly. "The two of you will have to work that out on your own, but I realized I was preaching to myself as much as to her. I might have to do the same thing—trust in people's basic goodness again. I have some painful memories here, but leaving you—Sawyer, that's going to hurt more."

Sawyer met her gaze seriously. "Tell me you're staying."

"I'm...thinking about it. It kind of depends," she said, swallowing.

"On what?" he asked softly. "Name it."

"On...you."

Sawyer's face cracked into a grin. "Well, I've been told off by my uncle, and he made a few good points. I work too hard, number one."

Olivia laughed softly. "Yeah, we all know that."

"And number two, I need to relax a bit and follow my heart."

Olivia sucked in a breath, waiting for his next words, but they didn't come. She eyed him uncertainly.

"And?" she prodded.

"I thought that was obvious," he replied, dipping his head down to peck her lips. "It leads straight to you."

Olivia felt a rush of relief. "Oh, I'm glad…"

"Look, Olivia," he said seriously. "I'm not going to ask you stay here and just see how things go, because I know how I feel about you, and it's not going to change. More memories won't change what I have with you right here and now. I want to marry you. I want you to raise my girls with me. I want to come home to you, and go to church with you and needle Lloyd about his crush on Evelyn with you." He smiled ruefully at that last one.

Olivia looked up at him, stunned. The breeze blew a curl into her face, and she brushed it away, her mind spinning. He'd just proposed. Was this crazy? It had all happened so fast...except that it had been simmering in her heart for years. She loved this man, and she realized in that moment that this was what she wanted—a life with Sawyer on the ranch, a life in boots, with little kids and family around. Coming back to Beaut wouldn't be easy, but it would be worth it if she could do it with the man who filled her heart.

"I don't know if I could afford to move back, though," she confessed. "I'm already stretched thin with the hospital debt, and if I made less—"

"I could help out with that."

"That's too much—"

"Not if I'm asking you to marry me," he murmured, a smile tugging up at his lips.

"Are you really?" she whispered.

"Yeah. I am. I'll help you out. We'll do it together. We won't be rich, but we'll be happy. If that's enough for you."

"It is." She nodded, blinking back tears.

"So...?" Sawyer's breath was bated.

"Yes, I'll marry you—"

Sawyer kissed her again, his arms pulling her close as she leaned into his strong embrace. When he pulled back, he took her hand and nodded up toward the house.

"You want to go share our news?" he asked, his voice low.

"I think I do." She laughed, hugging his arm close against her. "But you know that crush Lloyd has on Evelyn?"

"Yeah?" They started walking together up the road hand in hand in that wash of lowering light.

"I'm pretty sure Evelyn feels the same way," Olivia said. "Just a feeling."

Maybe there would be more kids than just Bella and Lizzie running around the ranch soon. Maybe there would be a few of Olivia and Sawyer's babies, too...and if Lloyd and Evelyn decided to make a go of it, there could be all sorts of cousins and siblings to grow up together. There would be a new generation of kids to learn the hard lessons and to protect each other.

Beaut wasn't perfect, but there would be people here who were kinder than before. People who'd grown and needed a bit of grace. The one person who she could trust wholeheartedly had just asked her to marry him. She'd be okay. She'd be more than okay—she'd be Sawyer's wife and a mom to his two little girls. She'd stand by his side and fight just as valiantly as he did for their family. And she'd find the good in this town, for their sakes.

"I love you, Olivia," Sawyer said softly.

"I love you, too."

Home would be in Sawyer's arms, and God could help her sort out the rest.

Epilogue

Olivia stood in the judge's office, a bouquet of summer flowers clutched in her hands. She wore a simple white sundress, in keeping with their plan to make their wedding small and affordable. With the debt that Olivia and Brian still owed, they didn't have anything extra to put into wedding frills, but Olivia didn't mind. She was here with the man she loved, legally becoming his wife and mom to Bella and Lizzie… She didn't care about frills. She had everything she needed.

They'd brought along Brian, Shari, Lloyd and Evelyn to be their witnesses and to wrangle the toddlers during the ceremony.

She glanced over to see Bella sprinkling her sippy cup of milk over a potted plant, and she had to stop herself from chuckling.

"Olivia, it's time for you to say your vows," the judge said. "Repeat after me..."

And Olivia repeated the words the judge intoned: "I promise to be your wife, for better or for worse, in sickness and in health, for as long as we both shall live."

"And you, Sawyer," the judge said.

"I promise to be your husband, for better or for worse, in sickness and in health, for as long as we both shall live."

"And the rings..."

Olivia turned and handed the bouquet to Shari. Shari's pregnancy was already starting to show, her belly domed out in front of her and the engagement ring sparkling on her left hand.

As Olivia and Sawyer exchanged rings, her heart swelled. This was going to be her husband, the man she clung to, supported, loved and respected for the rest of her days. Whatever life threw at them, they'd get through it.

Sawyer had married her, debt and all. He'd said that it didn't matter to him. He'd rather have her at his side and let God take care of the details. He loved her that much, and she was that blessed.

Olivia slid Sawyer's ring onto his finger, and he did the same for her—a simple golden band. She'd forgone an engagement ring because of the expense, but this ring was the one that mattered most. It meant that they belonged to each other...finally.

"With the power vested in me by the state of Montana, I now pronounce you husband and wife," the judge said.

Olivia met Sawyer's gaze and a smile erupted on his face. He pulled her into his arms and his lips came down over hers. She sighed against him. He was well and truly hers.

"And as a wedding gift from the town of Beaut..." the judge said, clearing his throat. "When you're done, of course."

There was humor in the older man's voice, and Olivia could hear the clapping and laughter of their invited guests. Lizzie squeezed up between them so that they had to break off the kiss. Sawyer scooped the toddler up into his arms, and they turned back to the judge.

"What do you mean?" Olivia asked.

"Some of your friends have taken up a collection," the judge said. "It was understood that you and your brother are in debt because of your mother's hospital bills."

Olivia looked over her shoulder to where Brian stood behind Shari's chair. His expression showed he was equally surprised by this turn in the conversation.

"Yes, but we're working on that," Olivia said quickly.

"Well, as a wedding gift, Lloyd took it upon himself to talk to the rest of community about helping you out. We've taken up a collection to help with the bills. We managed to collect forty-seven thousand dollars towards your debt."

Olivia's heart hammered in her chest. "People just gave it?" she whispered. "I don't know how to thank everyone… It's just so generous!"

She turned toward Lloyd, who was scuffling his boot into the carpet uncomfortably. "Well…we do what we can. It wasn't just my idea. A lot of people thought it would be the right thing to do."

"It doesn't cover all of your bill," the judge went on, "so Senator White spoke with the hospital board and got the amount owed lowered considerably, then he offered to top up the last of the money owing. Olivia… Sawyer… Brian… Your debt is paid."

Tears welled in Olivia's eyes and she put a hand over her mouth. Paid. In full. The debt that had been crushing them for years was now gone, and she and Sawyer could start their married life free of that burden. Brian could marry Shari without those payments sucking away his livelihood. His extra money could go toward his baby instead… and maybe to that business he wanted to start so badly.

"Brian," she said, spinning around. "We're

debt-free!" Olivia squeezed her husband's hand and looked up at him in amazement. "Did you know about this, Sawyer?"

"Nope," he said. Tears sparkled in his eyes, too. "But it just goes to show that kindness can be a group effort. We'll find a way to thank everyone."

Olivia and Sawyer ended up taking out an ad in the local newspaper. In it was a picture from their wedding showing Olivia snuggled up next to Sawyer, the toddlers in their arms, and tears sparkling in their eyes.

"We cannot thank you enough for your kindness," the ad said. "You are the good in the world. Thank you for changing ours! From the West family."

And for Wyatt and Irene, they did the one thing that would fill the older couple's hearts—they invited them over for a family dinner. It wasn't about the money—this was part of the plan anyway, but they wanted to acknowledge what Irene and Wyatt had done for them. It would be the cautious beginning of a long family relationship, where

Mia's parents were finally able to be a part of their granddaughters' lives. They'd overstep sometimes, and there were a few hard feelings over the years, but the Whites and the Wests were quick to apologize and quick to forgive, because they knew what mattered more than pride, and that was family.

Sawyer did get back his memory in full. It took a few months for all the details to come back to him, and the more he remembered, the more grateful he became for Olivia. Life hadn't been easy to get them here, but Olivia could feel God's grace surrounding them, making life sweet. This was what grace looked like in practice, Olivia would realize again and again…a mishmash of family. And it filled their hearts to the brim.

* * * * *

Dear Reader,

This is the last story in my Montana Twins miniseries, and I hope you've enjoyed the ride. If you just picked this book up and you like Montana-raised cowboys and adorable twins, you might want to pick up the two previous books, too.

You can find me online at PatriciaJohnsRomance.com. I'm also on Facebook and Twitter where I keep you up to date on my new releases and give you a view into my life. I'd love to hear from you!

Patricia Johns